mark timlin

the
turnaround

The Fifth Nick Sharman Thriller

NO EXIT PRESS

This edition published in 2014
by No Exit Press,
an imprint of Oldcastle Books
P.O.Box 394, Harpenden,
Herts, AL5 1XJ, UK

noexit.co.uk
@NoExitPress

First published in 1991 by Headline Book Publishing plc

ISBN
978-1-84344-269-1 (print)
978-1-84344-270-7 (epub)
978-1-84344-271-4 (kindle)
978-1-84344-272-1 (pdf)

Typeset by Avocet Typeset, Somerton, Somerset
in 11 on 13.5pt Garamond
Printed in Great Britain by Clays Ltd, St Ives plc
For more information about Crime Fiction go to crimtetime.co.uk
@CrimeTimeUK

This book is for Patrick Timlin

Acknowledgements
Arms Consultant: Nigelle de Bar.

We live in a sad land,
where only the ghosts are good.

1

I was sitting in my office watching morning TV on a little black and white portable with a 3 screen and a speaker with about as much definition as a piece of string and a tin can. I had my heels up on the edge of the desk and was nibbling on a raisin Danish and drinking a cup of tea. I was tuned into one of those magazine programmes where well-intentioned people in the know tell us mere mortals how to run our lives and make the perfect Bolognese sauce. This particular expert was a narrow-faced individual with a flop of pale hair that tumbled over his forehead in casual disarray that probably took the hairdresser at the studio an hour to arrange. The expert was telling me, and half a million or so other housewives and unemployed, how to get the best out of our hormone replacement therapy. I was making mental notes.

After the minute or so allowed for the item, in case us daytime couch potatoes got bored and switched over to the school broadcast on BBC2, the disgustingly clean-cut and happily married couple who presented the show popped up to tell us that a fifty-year-old, self-proclaimed celibate, but reputedly gay, pop star who'd just married a sixteen-year-old ex-convent schoolgirl at a beach front ceremony in St Lucia, was joining us for coffee to explain his mid-life change. After the break. I never got the lowdown. During an ad for panty-shields, the door of my office opened. Standing on the threshold was a young middle-aged man with thinning brown hair, dark glasses, a boxer's broken nose riding sidesaddle on his face, and an expensive trench coat. He looked at me. I looked at him, kept my heels on the desk and chewed on a raisin.

'Busy?' he asked.

'So-so,' I replied.

'Nice work if you can get it.' He had a South London accent. Sharp and hard.

I swallowed the raisin, brought my heels down on to the dusty rug behind my desk and hit the off button on the TV, brushed the cake crumbs off my jeans and said, 'Can I help you or are you just passing through?' These days I don't even make a pretence of being polite to uninvited callers.

'You're Sharman?'

'That's me.'

'Good. I'd like you to help me.'

Was this guy serious? I had difficulty helping myself at a buffet lunch. What did he think I could do for him? 'Is that a fact?' I said.

'Yes.'

'I don't know,' I said.

'That's what you do, isn't it? Help people.'

'Sometimes they don't think so,' I said. 'Not when it's all over.'

'I'll be the judge of that.'

I didn't say anything.

'Well?' he said.

'I don't know,' I said again, and looked longingly at the TV. 'I've got a few things on.'

'Yes,' he replied. 'I can see business is booming.'

'You're witnessing a quiet moment in a busy life.'

'I bet.' He took off his glasses. There was something in his eyes.

Something I didn't want to see. 'Well?' he asked.

I relented. It was the look in his eyes that did it. 'Sit down.'

He took off his coat and hung it on a hook on the wall. He pulled up a chair and sat down. Close up he didn't look so good. Underneath his expensive coat he was wearing an expensive suit, but it hung on him like he'd recently lost a lot of weight. And the collar of his shirt was wrinkled where he'd pulled his tie tight to hide the fact that it was at least half a size too big for him. His eyes were sunken with dark circles under them. His skin was grey and I could count the pores around his nose.

I lit a Silk Cut and finished my tea. I didn't offer him a cup. If he was interesting the pub over the road had just opened. If he wasn't, it was a waste of a tea bag. 'What can I do for you?' I asked.

'Find out who murdered my sister.'

'Your sister?'

'And her family.'

I mulled over that for a moment. 'You'd better tell me what happened,' I said.

He closed his eyes and rubbed the top of his broken nose with the forefinger and thumb of his right hand. He sighed deeply and started. 'Just over a year ago – March twenty-eighth last, to be exact – my sister, her husband and their two sons were murdered in their house in Crown Point. They were shot in cold blood.'

'I remember that,' I said. 'The Hellermann family.'

'Kellerman,' he corrected me.

'That's it,' I said. 'Haven't the police got anyone for it?'

'The police!' He almost spat. 'After twelve months the team investigating the murder had been run down to a detective sergeant and a woman PC. Now the superintendent in charge has retired to Southern Ireland and the incident room's closed. As of yesterday the investigation's over.'

'Murder investigations are never over.'

'This one might just as well be. There were forty people on the case the week after it happened and now there's no one.'

'Manpower,' I said.

'Manpower, my arse.'

I felt that we were getting nowhere. 'What can I do that the police can't?' I asked. It seemed like a reasonable question.

'Find out who killed Sandy.'

'Sandy?'

'Sandra. That was my sister's name.'

'Mr…?' I said with a query in my voice.

'Webb. James Webb. Call me Jim or Jimmy.'

'Mr Webb,' I said. 'There was a lot of publicity after the case, wasn't there? It was on *Crimewatch* if I remember rightly.'

He nodded.

'If the police couldn't come up with anything with – what was it? – forty men, did you say?' He nodded again. 'And the BBC behind them, what can I hope to find? And it has been nearly fourteen months.'

'Sharman,' said James Webb, 'you're well known round here. You've done well. People say that if anyone can dig something up, it's you.'

I was flattered. But not a lot. 'Listen, Mr Webb,' I said, 'I don't really think I can help you. Besides, it seems kind of dangerous to me.'

'You scared?'

I nodded. 'Every day of my life.'

'Couldn't you try?' he asked.

'I'm expensive.'

'So am I, Mr Sharman. My sister was all the family I had. Apart from my wife, of course,' He added her as an afterthought. 'But we have no children. Sandra and David and the boys were my family. I've got a photo here.' He pulled out his wallet, and from that a postcard-sized photograph. He handed it to me. It was a holiday snap. Unposed. Four people by a swimming pool. Two adults and two children. They were all perched on some kind of beach chair that seemed in danger of imminent collapse. The man looked tough. He was balding, but his body was covered in dark hair. The woman looked enough like James Webb to tell that they were related. But she was beautiful. Blonde and beautiful. Luckily the two children favoured her. Not that it mattered much now. They were light-haired and husky and both looked like they had just stopped or were just about to start laughing. It was one of the saddest things I've ever seen.

'I'm sorry,' I said.

'Are you?' He seemed surprised.

'Yes. I have a daughter of my own, not much older than those two. I know how I'd feel.'

'Then keep the photo and find out who killed them. I'm at my wit's end. I don't know which way to turn. I would have done anything for them. Now they're gone I have nothing left but my business. It's worth nothing to me now. I'm prepared to spend to find out who killed them.'

'I could just take your money and do nothing.'

I won't say he laughed. Whatever it was he did do, there was no humour in it. 'That's something else people say about you. You're straight with your clients.'

'I am,' I said.

'That's good enough for me. How much?'

'Two hundred a day plus expenses. And I might need to lay out some cash. It's funny how some people won't talk to the police but will get extremely vocal at the picture of the Queen on a fifty pound note or three.'

'Do what you have to.'

'No receipts, I'm afraid. Those same people can hardly remember their names most days.'

'I don't care about that.'

I put the photograph he'd given me carefully on the top of my desk. 'All right, Mr Webb, I'll give it a try. I'll do what I can on one condition.'

'Which is?'

'If it's pointless, I quit. I won't waste your money and I won't waste my time.'

'That sounds fair enough.'

'Good,' I said. 'You'd better fill me in on all the details. I don't suppose you fancy a drink?'

2

He did as it happened, and we went over to the pub. He paid. I had a bottle of lager. He had an orange juice. We sat at a table in the corner out of the way. I lit a cigarette. He told me he'd given up years before. I told him I had too, several times.

He sipped at his juice and I said, 'You were going to tell me what happened.'

'Yes,' he said in reply. He looked longingly at my cigarettes and started: 'My brother-in-law owned a couple of carpet warehouses just outside London. One in Croydon, one near Gatwick. The Intercontinental Carpet Company it was called. You might have heard of it.' I hadn't, but I didn't say. 'He seemed to be doing well. He had plans to open another two or three on the coast. Then the recession started to bite, so he shelved the plans. But he still seemed to be doing fairly well. He was a good husband. He loved my sister and she loved him.

'One night, the twenty-eighth of March last year, like I said, about ten o'clock as far as we can tell, somebody got into their house at Crown Point. It's a big house, set in its own grounds. It's called Oakfield. My sister and Dave were watching TV in the lounge at the back of the house. Whoever did it smashed one of the patio doors to get in. They shot the pair of them, and then went upstairs and shot my two nephews. One in the hall, one in bed. They had no chance. They were only babies. The bastards used shotguns on them.' He clutched at his glass and his eyes were wet. 'Then after they were killed, I found out that the business was in trouble.'

'Did he owe money?' I asked.

'Some, but the Nat West don't usually send gunmen to collect.'

'How much?'

'Half a million quid.' Not bad, I thought. Even these days half a million is hardly chickenfeed.

'Any private debts?'

'Nothing's turned up.'

'So what exactly was wrong with the business at the end?'

He blew out softly between pursed lips. 'What wasn't? The usual. Cash flow. Interest on the bank loan. No sales. New stock ordered before the slump came, to replace stuff that wasn't sold. No cancellation clause. The warehouse was full and the tills were empty. Too many overheads. Rent, wages… Christ, it never stopped.'

'So what's happened to it now?'

'It's gone. I put it into the hands of the receivers not long after he died. I didn't want to do it, but I had no choice.'

I made a sympathetic noise. 'To get back to that night,' I said. 'Didn't the neighbours hear anything?'

He shook his head. 'There's not that many houses around. It's an exclusive area. The back looks over the park. No one heard or saw a thing. Whoever it was vanished into thin air.'

'Was there an alarm on the place?'

'Alarms. Christ, the place was rotten with them. They even had panic buttons installed. There was one in the room where they were killed.'

'But they didn't use it?'

He shook his head.

'So it looks like they could have known the people.'

'It does. Or they were overpowered before they could get to them.'

'But if they *did* know them,' I said, 'why did they bother to break in? The panic buttons *were* working?'

He nodded.

'Where were the patio doors? In the same room as where they were killed?'

'Yes.'

'Seems a bit strange. Who found them?'

'A neighbour. Mrs Godbold. Out with her dog. The front door was open.'

'They came in the back and out the front. I wonder why they did that?'

'That's for you to find out.'

I ignored the comment. 'And the police have still got no leads?' I said.

'None.'

'It's going to be bloody difficult.'

'But you will do it?'

'I'll do my best,' I said.

'Thank you.' He took a cheque book out of his pocket and started writing out a cheque. 'A thousand do you?'

A thousand always does me. 'Thanks,' I said.

He finished writing out the cheque, folded it and put it next to my glass. 'Where will you start?'

'The police. What station handled it? Gipsy Hill?'

He nodded.

Gipsy Hill Street Blues, I thought. 'What was the name of the officer in charge?'

'Superintendent Meadows.'

I shook my head. 'Don't know him.'

'He's gone anyway,' said Webb. 'Retired to Ireland like I told you. There was an Inspector Robber I spoke to.'

'Jack Robber,' I said. 'Christ, Robber by name…'

'What does that mean?'

'It means everybody else does the work and he steals the glory.'

'You know him then?'

'I know of him.'

'There wasn't much glory to be had in this case.'

'That wouldn't please him.'

'So he won't be friendly to you?' asked Webb.

'Not many coppers round here are.'

'But I thought you used to be a copper yourself.'

'All the more reason.'

'Maybe you should move.'

'To Mars?'

'That bad?'

'I'll survive. But it doesn't help you much. I warn you, I won't get much cooperation. So if you want to leave it…' I pushed the cheque back across the smeary top of the table.

He waved it away. 'No. The coppers haven't done much. Maybe you can.'

I shrugged.

'What exactly will you do?' he asked.

'Ask questions. Nose and listen, Mr Webb.'

'Jim.'

'Jim.' Now I had his cheque I supposed it was OK to call him that. We were war veterans by then. Buddies. 'I'm going into a cold case. Very cold,' I said. 'I don't know what I'm going to find. It might be nothing, it might be bad.'

'Whatever.'

'All right. Now what about the house?'

'What about it?'

'What have you done with it?'

'It's locked up.'

'Empty?'

He nodded.

'Who does it belong to?'

'Me. Everything passed to me by default. There was no other family. I was going to put the house up for sale but the estate agent said we should leave it until people began to forget. It's not exactly a selling point, and a bunch of ghouls would pretend to be interested just to get a look inside.'

'Was it paid for?'

'No. But there was insurance. You know, linked to the mortgage. That paid off the building society.'

'No other insurance?'

'No. David cashed those in.'

'When?'

'Not long before. When the business was first in trouble.'

'And you didn't need the proceeds from selling the house to pay off the bank loan on the business?'

'I'm not short, I told you that.'

Obviously, I thought. 'So you just left it?'

He nodded. 'And then someone broke in.'

'When?'

'About two months after the murders.'

'What did they get?'

'Nothing.'

'I see,' I said. I didn't, but maybe it was important, or maybe it was some of Webb's ghouls looking for kicks.

'What did they do?'

'Turned the place over. Made a mess. I had to go and clear it up myself. My wife won't go there.'

I wasn't surprised. I wasn't exactly looking forward to going myself. But I knew I'd have to. 'Have you got a spare set of keys?' I asked.

'Of course.'

'Can I borrow them?'

'You want to go there?'

I nodded. 'Visit the scene of the crime. Get some atmosphere.'

He didn't look too happy about that.

'I'm not going for fun,' I said.

'All right,' he said. He took a large bunch of keys out of the pocket of his coat, split off a ring with four keys on it, and passed them to me. 'The gates are padlocked. The front door's got a Yale and a Chubb lock.'

'Are the alarms on?'

He nodded.

'What kind?'

'Chubb.'

'Were they on when the place got done?'

'No.'

'Why not?'

'The police were in and out for weeks. I never bothered.'

'But you do now?'

He nodded again. 'Not that there's anything worth stealing.'

'But just in case.'

'Yes. If the police want to go in now, they have to make an appointment. Not that they ever do,' he added bitterly.

'How do the alarms work?'

'Simple. From the moment you turn the main key in the front door – the Chubb – a buzzer sounds. Then you've got thirty seconds to punch the number code on the key pad just inside the door. On the right,' he added. 'On the way out you push the "set" button, the buzzer sounds again and you've got thirty seconds to turn the key and lock the door.'

'I'll sort it out,' I said. 'Give me the numbers.'

'I'll come with you if you like.'

'No,' I said. 'I'd rather go alone. I work better that way.'

He nodded and took a notebook out of his pocket and wrote down a series of numbers, tore out the page and gave it to me. I glanced at it and put it in my pocket. 'I'll go in the morning,' I said.

'Why not today?'

'There's one more condition to taking the case,' I said.

'What?'

'I do it my way or not at all.'

'Of course. I'm sorry, it's just…'

'I need to talk to people first,' I said. 'Get some idea of what's happened in the past fourteen months, and if possible before. Besides, what's another day matter?'

'You're right. Do you want another drink?'

I nodded and he went to the bar. When he got back I said, 'What do you do, Jim?'

'It says company director on my passport.'

'What kind of company?'

'Companies. All sorts. Import-export, buying and selling. Anything that'll turn a profit. I've been successful. I was a boxer.' He touched his nose self-consciously. 'Not a very good one, but I had a good manager. He taught me to hold on to my money. It was him started me off. Sports gear. Then skateboards about fifteen years ago. We made a killing and got out before the bottom dropped out of the market. But I kept importing the clothes. I was one of the very first people to bring American trainers into this country. They became fashionable, I coined it.'

'Nice,' I said.

He shrugged. 'Like I told you, it don't mean nothing to me now.'

We sipped at our drinks for something to do apart from talk about death again. 'What now?' he asked.

'I'm going to think. You get back to your life. Leave this to me, all right?'

'All right.'

'Give me your number before you go,' I said. 'I'll be in touch.'

He gave me a pasteboard card with phone number and an address in Crystal Palace printed on it in discreet gold lettering. 'I mostly work from home now,' he said. 'You'll usually get me there.'

I had a feeling he didn't do much but sit around the house all day thinking about his sister and her family. 'Thanks,' I said. 'I'll remember that.'

We drank up and left. He was driving a dark blue Daimler with a current registration. Not bad. He sounded the horn as he drove off. I went back to the office and made some more tea.

3

I put on the TV again. Then shook my head, switched it off and telephoned Gipsy Hill police station. 'Police,' said a voice.

'Is Inspector Robber there?'

'Who's speaking?'

'Nick Sharman.'

'Concerning?'

'Personal,' I said.

I was put through. 'Robber,' said a gruff voice.

'My name's Sharman,' I said. 'Nick Sharman.'

'*The* Nick Sharman?'

'The only one I know.'

'I am honoured,' he said. 'What's up? Do you want a couple of tickets to the policeman's ball?' And he laughed an ugly laugh.

'No,' I said. 'James Webb has hired me to look into the murder of his brother-in-law and his family.'

There was a long pause. He obviously wished I had. 'You're wasting your bloody time,' said Robber. 'And mine.'

'Maybe so. But I wonder if we could meet?'

'You've got a nerve, Sharman. I'll say that for you.' He paused again. 'Well, maybe. I've always wanted to meet someone who can kill a copper and get away with it.'

I said nothing in reply.

'Do you know The Three Hens at Crystal Palace?' he asked.

'The Bucket of Blood, you mean,' I said.

'You do know it. I'll be in the back bar at eight.'

'I'll see you then,' I said and put down the phone.

Oh Christ, I thought, The Three Hens. It was famous for being about the most horrible pub in an area where horrible pubs were the norm. A heavy metal and strippers pub that had closed down, changed hands, been refurbished and made more come-backs than Frank Sinatra.

I parked my car about three streets away from the pub at 7.45. I didn't want the Jag anywhere near the place. Some of the punters at The Hens would have had it stripped down and in the Middle East by breakfast time.

I wore old jeans, an older leather jacket, a denim shirt and running shoes in case I had to beat a quick retreat. I took no wallet or ID, just a few fivers in the watch pocket of my jeans, a packet of cigarettes and a box of matches. I zipped my car keys into one of the pockets of my jacket and I was ready. The pub was at the end of a narrow street and the car park looked down Anerley Hill. Not that anyone used the car park. Not for parking cars anyway. The street was deserted and deathly quiet, and the sodium lamps sizzled audibly in the damp air. There were half a dozen big motor bikes lined up at the kerb outside the boozer like guards.

I went through the first door I came to, pushed aside a set of heavy velvet curtains and got hit over the head with a blast of *Bohemian Rhapsody* at top volume. The place was packed with leather jackets, jeans, Spandex leggings, boots and hair. Lots of hair. Flat tops, long curls, ponytails and bouffants. There was a drum kit with enough cymbals to ring in the second coming on a high stage in one corner. In front of the stage was a smaller one and on it was a hard-faced momma dressed in high-heeled red shoes, stockings, suspenders and half a basque. The rest of the basque was hanging down exposing spectacular, if rather droopy, breasts with big brown nipples. I imagined she was about the age of most of the average punters' mothers. I felt sorry for her parading that tired old flesh for the umpteenth time. I knew how I'd feel.

There was a geezer with more barnet than enough in a leather suit spinning records to one side of the larger stage. He segued from *Queen* to *Metallica* with a flick of his wrist. The stripper threatened to expose more cellulite and I made for a sign that read BACK BAR followed by an arrow. It was a bit quieter in there, but not much. The bar contained a CD jukebox and Jon Bon Jovi was giving it plenty through speakers the size of small packing cases. I pushed through the crowd to where there was a clear gap of four feet or more in front of a round table and two chairs. One of the chairs was occupied by a big, grey-haired geezer in a dirty tan mac. He was drinking a pint and chewing on a pork pie as if he was alone in the snug of a quiet country pub and *Bon Jovi* was just a dream. I went over to him. 'Mr Robber?' I said.

'Sharman?'

I nodded.

He pointed at his glass. 'Pint of John Smith's.'

I pushed back through the crowd to the bar. 'A pint of Smith's and what bottled beer you got?' I'd seen the state of the pots in the pub before, but if you asked for a clean glass they thought you were a cissy.

'Becks, Heineken,' said the barman.

'Becks,' I said. 'No glass.'

'No glass, no beer, mate,' he said with a sneer.

'All right,' I said, and watched him pour the liquid from the bottle into a cloudy glass. I took Robber's and my drink back to the table. He'd finished his pie. There were crumbs and a cellophane wrapper on the table. He swept them to the floor with his hand and finished the drink in front of him with one swallow.

I sat down and lit a cigarette and he snapped his fingers at me until I offered him one. Endearing trait, that.

'Your local?' I asked.

'What do you think?'

I looked at the backs of the people in the bar. 'Friendly,' I said.

'They don't want to come too close in case some of the policeman rubs off.'

'I know the feeling,' I said.

'Do you fuck,' he said back and pointed a dirty, fat finger at me. 'Don't talk about the job to me. You've given up the right.' He was well pissed off and I could hardly blame him.

'Fair enough,' I said. 'Can we talk about the Kellerman case then?'

'I told you, you're wasting your time.'

'Why?'

'Because, you stupid sod, if we couldn't find out who killed the poor bastards, how the hell do you think you can?'

I shrugged. The collar on his shirt was rimed with black, and his tie was stringy and worn through to the lining where it had been tied too many times. I wondered what he did with his money. He was on a good screw as a DI. Booze, fags and pork pies, I supposed. He probably had to pay for sex though. I don't know why that suddenly occurred to me.

'I could use some help,' I said.

It's at that point, on TV, that the kind copper hands the handsome PI the police files and tells him, with a wink, not to get caught looking at them. Smiles are exchanged and you just know that it will all work out in the end. Some fat chance, I thought. He never said a word.

'Listen, Mr Robber,' I said, 'I just want to know what happened.'

'Bollocks.'

I sighed and sipped at my glass at the opposite side to a smear of pale pink lipstick. It wasn't my shade. The jukebox began to churn out *Poison* doing some ripped off twelve-bar blues. I tried again. 'Why do you think they were killed?' I asked.

He drank more beer, took another of my cigarettes and decided to relent a little. 'Same reasons as always,' he said. 'Sex or money, or both.'

'And in this case?'

He shook his head. 'We couldn't find a thing.'

'He was going broke, wasn't he?'

Robber nodded.

'Was he into a shark?'

'He didn't need to be. He had good credit.'

'He was paying a lot of interest.'

'Him and a million other businessmen. It's a hard world out there. He was making do. Maybe he wouldn't have lasted a lot longer, who knows? But there didn't seem to be any other debts. Not that we could find. And we're pretty thorough as you know.'

'So if not money,' I said, 'sex then? Was he having it off? Or her?' I added.

'If one of them was, he or she was doing a good job of keeping it dark.'

'How about at work? His secretary? I imagine he had one.'

'He did, but not her. She's a raspberry ripple. Funny little thing, all twisted up and in a wheelchair. Stupid too. Fucking spastics.'

Jesus, but Robber was a depressing sod. Spastics, cripples, poofs, wogs, wops, women... I knew his sort. Anyone to insult and look down on. Iranians, Albanians, niggers, Pakis... just so he could feel good in his own bloody misery. What he didn't realise was that we're all shit in the same gutter. Ah, but some of us are looking at the stars.

'What was her name?' I asked.

'Natalie, Natalie Hooper. But I'm telling you, you're wasting your time there.'

I was beginning to get a headache. 'Why didn't one of them use the panic button they had in the room?'

'Because they must have known the people who killed them.'

'But they bust the door down to get in.'

'Did they?'

'So maybe they didn't?' I said.

'Maybe.'

'So you think they actually let them in through the front door?'

'They might have.'

He wasn't giving much away and my headache was getting worse. But at least he was talking. So I kept on, 'What makes you say that?'

'No footprints in the garden. It was damp weather, though not actually raining. No mud on the carpet. Then they went out the front way. One set of gates to the drive were wide open. We found two or three sets of tyre tracks on the drive that didn't match the Kellerman cars or any cars that belong to regular visitors. The Kellermans didn't use the panic button, nor did the kids. But we know they knew how. In fact, it's possible they killed the kids first. I reckon they wanted something from the Kellermans they didn't get. Someone came back later and spun the drum. It all adds up.'

'Yeah, but you don't know…'

Then he remembered who he was and who I was. 'I don't know much, Sharman,' he said. 'But I do know I've had it up to here with you. I've already told you more than I should and I'm tired. I've had enough of being a policeman today.'

The beat from the jukebox was relentless and thumped around the inside of my head like a hammer. 'I'm not surprised,' I said. 'Why do you come in here?'

He grinned evilly. 'To spoil their fucking fun,' he said, gesturing at the crowd. 'This place used to be rotten with dope. Now it's not.'

In your dreams, I thought. But if it gives you pleasure. 'Sort of a hobby?' I said.

'Beats stamp collecting.'

We sat in as much silence as we could muster, which wasn't much, for a minute. 'I'll tell you one thing for nothing, Sharman,' he said. 'Then you can go.'

'What?'

'Webb and Kellerman, they're both dirty. I fucking know it.'

'How dirty?'

'Don't ask me. We dug and dug and found nothing. But they are, believe me.'

I looked at him hard. 'Do you think Webb did it?'

Robber shrugged. 'He inherited.'

'Not much, from what I can gather. Besides, he didn't strike me as a mass murderer.'

'There's people around who are. For the right incentive.'

'And then he hires me fourteen months later, when the case is almost forgotten and the enquiry all but wound up?'

He interrupted me furiously. 'Murder's never forgotten. Never. And the case will never be closed.'

'Sure,' I said. But I knew, and he knew I knew. And all the denying in the world wouldn't make it any different. 'But why hire me now? He knows it's going to stir up a load of shit.'

He shrugged again.

'But you're convinced he knows more than he's telling?'

'That's about it,' he said. 'And you're right about shit. There's someone out there, probably two or more, who've tasted blood. It can be addictive. If you get close they might decide to see you off too. You wouldn't be missed much from what I can gather. So I'd check out of it if I were you, Sharman, before you bite off more than you can chew.'

He shook his head, as if I was mentally defective. 'Now fuck off and leave me alone. And take these with you.' He reached into the poacher's pocket of his mac, took out a brown envelope and passed it to me.

The files, I thought. Christ! But it wasn't. It was a slippery pile of 10 x 8, monochrome, scene-of-crime photos.

'Look at them,' he said, in such a way I couldn't refuse.

They were photos of horror caught in the harsh white light of a flash bulb. Highlights heightened. Shadows darkened. Faces turned into masks by death and the camera. Blood made black like spilt ink. Photo 1: Two bodies tumbled like dead insects. Heads half gone. Limbs shredded. Photo 2: Same scene from a different angle. A man and a woman lying together, him half on top of her. Pornography of a different kind. Photo 3: A hallway. A boy of about ten in pyjamas sprawled untidily on the floor. His eyes open and a gaping wound where his chest used to be. Photo 4: A bedroom. Half on and half off the bed, another dead boy. Maybe six years old this time. A strong resemblance to the other child. The bedclothes dark with blood and on the pillow next to the boy's head, a teddy bear. I flipped through the rest. Variations of the same horror. Not much like the happy family holiday snap Webb had given me.

I put the photos back in their envelope and tasted old beer, sharp and acid in my throat.

'Keep and enjoy,' said Robber. 'You didn't get them from me. Now get out of here.'

I stood up. 'Have a nice evening,' I said.

'Come round any old time. I'm always here.' And he laughed, showing dirty teeth with a piece of pie crust lodged between a molar and the next tooth.

'I'll remember that,' I said. I went back into the music bar where a bad imitation of *Bad Company* were doing *Can't Get Enough*.

I'm afraid I couldn't agree. I'd had more than enough for one evening. I went back to the Jag and drove home and my ears were ringing all the way.

I put the envelope in a drawer and made a decent drink of vodka and chocolate milk and smoked five cigarettes, one after another, and wondered what the hell I was getting into. A thousand pounds. Five days and finish.

I went to bed and lay there thinking about what Robber had said about James Webb. Dirty… or was he?

Surely not. If he was, why hire me at this late date? It didn't make sense. But what did? And with that thought, I fell asleep and dreamt of blood.

4

The next morning I made my first visit to the murder scene in Crown Point. I got up early and gave Cat his breakfast and made myself a bacon sandwich on whole-wheat toast and a cup of coffee. Cat and I didn't speak as we ate. I like that in breakfast companions. Some I've had never stop. I smoked a cigarette and listened to the news on the radio, let the cat out and set off.

It wasn't a long drive, barely fifteen minutes. But the part of Crown Point I wanted was one of those inner suburbs that has pretensions to being a village within a city. It probably hadn't changed much from when it *was* almost a village. And no one had bothered to put up any street signs. I had to double back and forth down avenues with no kerbs or pavements, lined with high walls or hedges, before I found the close I was looking for. There wasn't a living thing to be seen. It was like someone had come along and doped all the inhabitants. Not even a bird sang. I felt like the last person alive on the planet. Now that *would* be just my luck.

It was cloudy and cool when I stopped the car outside one of a pair of imposing iron gates set in the high walls around the house. They were closed tight and secured with a thick chain and padlock. I climbed out of the car and took the bunch of keys that James Webb had given to me out of my jacket pocket.

It was a Chubb lock, top of the range, and I found the appropriate key on the ring and tried it. It worked smoothly. I pulled the chain through and looped it over a curlicue of black iron and pushed one half of the gate open. It creaked as it parted from its mate. A real Hammer House of Horror job. I closed the gate behind me and crunched across the gravel drive towards the house. Grass was growing through the stones and the front garden was untidy and neglected. It was very quiet behind the garden walls with only the buzz of a plane beginning its run into Gatwick to break the silence.

Close to the house the lawn and the drive were churned with ancient tyre tracks and I imagined what it must have looked like on the night of the murders. First to arrive would have been crime cars and ambulances, headlights on full beam to illuminate the front of the house and blue lights flashing lazily at synchronised beats per second. Figures would have cast long, narrow shadows and their faces, pale under uniform caps, would have been lit harshly in the bright light. The air would have been full of the splintered crackle of the static-punctuated voices on the radios. Next would have come the anonymous Cavaliers and Sierras of the CID, parked outside to save any tyre tracks the first cars on the scene hadn't obliterated. Then more plain saloons would have arrived: SOCO, forensic and fingerprint teams. At first light, vans full of uniformed men for the fingertip search of the grounds and the mini-vans of the dog-handlers. Finally a mobile HQ would have been towed in and parked slap bang in the middle of the drive and a canteen would have set up outside the gates. TV crews would have filmed the lads eating bacon sarnies and drinking cups of tea for want of something better to do. That night and the next day would have been the busiest, the area taped off and all sorts of coppers wandering about trying to look important. And then...

Well then, as the days and weeks went past, and the murders went cold, and more recent atrocities vied for the public's and media attention, one by one the cars and vans and the canteen would have vanished, and finally the HQ would have been towed off again, and the gates locked, and the investigation team run down, and finally disbanded altogether.

And now there was just me. God help us all.

The house itself looked like it was asleep. Dark and melancholy under the low cloud, with its windows closed against curious eyes. I climbed the stone steps to the porch. The front door was fully ten feet high and six feet wide, made of old timbers bound by iron. I took the piece of paper Webb had given me with the combination to the alarm on and unlocked the door, using two more of the keys on the ring. It opened like the jaws of a trap.

I heard a buzzer start, just like he'd said it would, and pushed the door all the way and looked on the wall to my right. There was a key pad at chest height and I punched in the digits Webb had written down. The buzzer stopped. Very efficient. I stood on the threshold and smoked a cigarette before I went any further. Eventually I walked into the hall, leaving the door open behind me. I sniffed and thought I smelt old gunpowder and blood and death. I wrinkled my nose in disgust.

I hit all six light switches mounted above the alarm pad. A central fixture and wall-mounted lamps sprang to life and the interior of the hall came into chilly view. I shivered. I'd been inside houses where sudden death had struck lots of times in my life, but for some reason this was the closest to death I'd ever felt. I walked across the hall to the furthest door and opened it. The room was dark but it felt big. I ran my hand down the wall inside the door, found another light switch and pushed it down. For one split second as the light came on I thought I saw ghostly figures and faces turn towards me but the room was empty. Inside the room I saw the first signs of violence. The big, pale pink leather sofa was stained brown and there were huge tears in the fabric as if a giant had taken a bite out of the material. The cushions were shredded and the filling that had burst out from the covers was stained brown too. It was the room in the first of the photographs. I looked away from the wounded sofa and up at the walls. A long smear of brown marred the wallpaper and, when I looked closely, I saw dozens of small holes from a round of buckshot. Some had been enlarged where the forensic team had dug out the shot for analysis.

Pink velvet curtains covered one wall floor to ceiling, and I found the pulley and opened them. Half of the patio window had been removed and plywood filled the gap. I looked through the other at the unkempt back garden that stretched away for two or three hundred yards. It had started raining, and the sight of it made me feel colder. I looked around again and saw fingerprint powder remains on every surface. On top of the fingerprint powder was over a year's accumulation of dust. The daylight, dim as it was, showed up the stains on the carpet. On the night of the murders, it must have been a regular blood swamp. The place didn't look as if it had been turned over. Webb had made a good job of putting it back together again.

I left the room and went upstairs. The master bedroom faced the top of the stairs. I went in. It was neat and the bed was made. Apart from the dust on the surfaces it looked ready for use. I walked out again. Along the corridor was another set of stains and more holes in the wall, but lower down this time. I was standing where the elder of the boys had been shot. He'd only been about four feet tall after all. I was beginning to realise that there were really sick people involved in this case. Sick or desperate, or both.

I went into the first of two smaller bedrooms. It was empty. I left it and went next door into another small bedroom. Of all the rooms in the house, it smelled most strongly of death. It was where the younger boy had died. In the centre of the room was a bare mattress and base. The mattress was ripped apart and stained with old blood and body fluids. I don't know what possessed

Webb to keep it. A reminder, I suppose, to keep the anger fresh. No wonder his wife wouldn't come to the house or an estate agent to show people round.

The walls of the room were covered with fading posters of sports and pop stars. *Bros* and Kylie were splattered with body fragments. A long sliver of dead tissue hung down from a team picture of Chelsea FC. I was surprised forensic had missed it. Maybe they had more than enough by then, and left a little for me. I touched it, and it crumbled and fell to the floor. I rubbed my finger tips together to get rid of the remains of the mummified flesh and my mouth filled with sour saliva which I swallowed with a grimace.

I knew there was no point in searching the place. Hundreds of pairs of hands and eyes must have been through everything. I hardly expected that I would turn up anything new. I went back downstairs and left the house, resetting the alarm and locking the front door behind me. I walked back down the drive and through the gates and fastened the chain with the padlock again. I sat in the car and listened to a phone-in on organic farming in the Home Counties and smoked another cigarette to get the taste of the place out of my mouth. After ten minutes or so I started the car and went to get a drink. On the way out of the close I passed a dark blue Mini coming in.

5

As I sat in a miserable pub on the south side of Crown Point, near Croydon, I realised that I'd have to go back and knock on some doors around the Kellerman house. Maybe someone had seen something they hadn't told the police.

But I wasn't going back again that day. The combination of the rain, the photos I'd seen the previous night and my visit to Oakfield that morning, had dulled my enthusiasm for the job. Not that there'd been that much to start with. I was beginning to wish I'd stayed in my office watching TV. I decided to drive home, make a couple of calls, leave the car and walk to my favourite bar and seek some like-minded company. More unemployable people who had nothing to do all day. Then after a few beers I was going to go home again, shower, change, and take my main squeeze out to dinner. Not that she was quite as main or as squeezable as she had been, but that's life.

As soon as I got in, I called Webb. 'Sharman,' I said when he answered.

'Have you found anything?' he asked. His voice was full of hope.

'No,' I replied. 'But I've been to the house.'

'And?'

'Nothing,' I said. 'But why haven't you cleared it out?'

'I don't want to.'

'Any particular reason?'

'You wouldn't understand.'

'Try me.'

'I'm not going to touch it again until I know who killed them. If I ever start to forget, I can go back and look around again. Do you understand that?'

Jesus Christ, I thought. 'I understand, Jim,' I said. It was the first time I'd called him that because I wanted to. 'Better than you'll ever know.' I didn't explain. It would have taken a lifetime. 'Listen, I'll get back to you. Call me if you need anything. You've got my number?'

'Yes.'

'OK. I'll see you.'

I got to the bar around two. There were a few faces in there that I knew. I drank three bottles of Rock and discussed the state of the world and daytime TV. The world came off worst. After I'd finished my third drink I left.

Fiona arrived at seven. One thing I will say is that she's punctual. She used her own key to let herself in. She was dressed in a long, dark blue coat over a lilac mini-dress in some material that stretched where she was convex and shrank where she was concave. It was an edifying sight.

'Hello, Nick,' she said as she came in.

'Hello yourself. How are you?'

'Just dandy. What's the plan?'

'Dinner at Lena's. My treat. Dawdle over coffee and liqueurs and back here. How does that grab you?'

'Fine,' she said and came over and kissed me briefly. 'Who's driving?'

'Cabbies. I've called a taxi. Ten minutes.'

It was nearer half an hour before the cabbie arrived and from the state of the motor it was a miracle he'd got there at all. He was driving a Morris Marina automatic that wouldn't kick itself out of low drive. The car was showing more smoke than the QE2. The radio was stuck on Capital Gold, and the back seat cushion wasn't attached to any other part of the car. Every time the Marina got up enough speed to warrant using the brakes, the bloody seat tipped forward and nearly left us on the carpet. Once Fiona and I would have had hysterics and held tightly to each other, choking with laughter, and the whole thing would have made our evening. Now it just made us both irritable.

When we got to Lavender Hill the driver asked for a fiver. I gave him three quid and dared him with a look to take it further. He left it.

We went inside the restaurant and got our favourite table in the corner by the window. I had a Singha beer to calm me down and Fiona had a gin. We started on the prawn crackers and things started to warm up a bit.

'I can sit on my hair,' she said after she'd sunk three-quarters of her large gin and tonic in one gulp. Her hair had got very long and hung over her shoulders and down her back as black and shiny as newly mined coal.

'You nearly sat on it in the back of that bloody cab,' I said.

'I know. Your face! It was a picture.'

'You kept showing your knickers to the driver,' I said. 'I wouldn't mind but I had to pay him *and* he got a show.'

'You're lucky I've got any on. Every time the seat tilted my skirt got caught up and I didn't. It wasn't my fault.'

I had to laugh and she joined in. 'Oh, Nick,' she said. 'You do try and stay dignified.'

'So?'

'And you just end up looking like your shoes hurt.'

'OK,' I said after a minute. 'You're right. Sorry, it's been a bad day.'

'Why?'

'I'm working on a new case.'

'What?'

I told her a bit. Not everything. I've found that murder and Thai food don't go. It can ruin the soft noodles if you're not careful. So, like I said, I told her a bit.

When I'd finished she said, 'Can't you get a proper job?'

I'd obviously told her too much.

'You knew what I was.'

'I know, but…'

'But you thought I'd change.' I finished her sentence for her. She pulled a face. We'd had similar conversations before.

'Let's not go into it again,' I said.

'OK, Nick.'

So somewhat subdued, but at least still friends, we ordered our food. By the time we'd eaten chicken satay, sweetcorn and crab meat in tiny savoury baskets, prawns in a black pepper sauce, stir-fried vegetables and a portion of special noodles with mixed meats; and drunk between us a bottle of wine, two gins, three beers, four of the best cappuccinos in London, and five liqueurs, we were less subdued and I got the waiter to order us a cab back to mine. I checked, just in case, but the restaurant didn't use the firm with the cab with the mobile back seat.

We got back about eleven. I turned the lights down low and put a Sam Cooke album on the stereo. Corny, but I did it anyway. Trouble is it's hard to be subtle in a studio flat when the largest item of furniture in the room is the bed. Not that Fiona and I were exactly strangers to it. But, you know, sometimes it's good not to be too predictable.

'Seduction, Sharman?' she asked. I needn't have bothered. She reads me like a book, see.

'Have a drink and shut up,' I said.

'You'll have me pissed.'

'Good.'

'I expect you've got some weed to get me horny too.'

'If you want,' I said. 'Someone gave me a few joints.'

'And if they gave out airline tickets down on the farm, pigs could fly.'

She got up to get a joint out of the drawer where I generally keep such things. 'What are these?' She held up the envelope full of the SOC photos at the Kellerman house that Robber had given to me.

'Don't,' I said.

She opened the flap and pulled out the photos. 'Jesus Christ,' she said as she riffled through them.

'I didn't want you to see those.'

'Nick, is this what you're involved in?'

I didn't answer. I didn't have to.

'Keep your drink, and your dope,' she said. 'I'm going.'

'Fiona –'

'No. Call me when you're out of it.' And she put on her coat and left. She was over the limit to drive but I didn't think that it was the right time to mention it.

I found one of the joints and lit up. I took Sam Cooke off the turntable and put on Herbie Hancock instead. With the volume very low. I kicked off my shoes and sat in front of the dead TV set and thought about Fiona and me. Me and Fiona. We'd been together for a while. Well, six or seven months anyway. Something of a record.

Then she'd got too involved in a case I was working on that ended in a spectacularly messy way. After it was all over she decided that I should settle down and get a 'proper job', as she called it. I refused and the relationship had started to splinter. The problem was that I knew she still loved me, and I loved her too. As much as I know how. Maybe that was the trouble. She recognised my lack of commitment and resented it. And who could blame her? Christ knows, I wanted to be committed to someone. But somehow it never seemed to happen. There's something lacking in me, see. Ask anyone. Especially my wife and the girlfriends I had before and since, and even at the same time.

I finished the joint and dropped the roach in the ashtray. The music was mellow. So was the dope. It was me that wasn't. I got up and wandered round the room. I lit a Silk Cut and poured Jack Daniel's over ice from the fridge. I stayed up late and finished the bottle. Don't get me wrong, there was only a drop. Eventually I went to bed and lay on my back and watched the wash of light from the car headlamps criss-cross the ceiling. It wasn't the way I'd planned the evening to end. But you can't always get what you want. Seems to me too often you get what you deserve.

Eventually I fell asleep.

6

The next morning I decided to go back to Crown Point and start doing a house to house in case the police had missed anything. It was a slim chance, but I had to do something. So I got up early again, fed Cat and then took myself to my favourite café in Norwood Road where I got double egg, bacon, sausage, tomatoes, baked beans, fried slice, tea, toast and heartburn all for a couple of quid. How bad? Refills of tea on demand. I took the *Telegraph* with me for the crossword. I did seven clues. Not good. I was too busy thinking about the Kellerman murders. I gave the paper to the cook, paid the bill, took a mint and walked back to get the car and drive to Crown Point again.

There was a silver Ford Escort parked opposite my house with two people sitting in the front. I clocked them as I got in the E-Type. Two blokes sitting well back so I couldn't see their faces. The car was a foreigner. It didn't belong in the area. When I was on the force I met villains who knew every car in their district. They could spot strange wheels at a quarter of a mile. It kept some of them out of nick for years. It's a lesson I've never forgotten.

I started the Jag and pulled out into the road and turned right. It was the long way round, but I wanted to see if they would follow me. They did. As I drove up towards Streatham, the Escort did a swift U-turn behind me. I drove through the avenues and headed west along the back streets. I stopped at the junction with Leigham Court Road, indicated left, turned right, causing a Thames van to skid broadside, turned sharp left into a narrow one-way street the wrong way, and accelerated down it, flashing my lights and forcing a Golf convertible on to the pavement. I turned left again, then right, and cut into Streatham High Road in front of a garbage truck, and the Escort was nowhere to be seen. So it looked like *someone* was coming out of the woodwork. I thought of the photos that Robber had given to me and shivered involuntarily.

Still I carried on. I got to the close about ten. There were five houses in sight of the Kellermans'. They all had reasonably extensive grounds and the immediate neighbours had high walls or fences separating them. But someone might have seen something.

And not told the police? Fat chance.

None of the houses was numbered. They all had names. The first one I tried was called Buck House. Very droll, I thought. There was no one at home but the au pair, an engaging girl from what I translated as one of the Benelux countries. I had to translate because she spoke not a word of English. So she wasn't much help.

Next: Psycho's Place. I swear to God. What the fuck were these people on? I rang the bell. A jolly-looking individual in a Marks and Sparks summer-weight cardie appeared at the door a moment later. I introduced myself. He looked vaguely interested, but didn't invite me in. 'I've been here less than a year, old mate,' he said. 'I can't help you, I'm afraid.'

'Thanks anyway,' I said, and turned to go. Then I turned back. 'Why do you call the house Psycho's Place?' I asked. 'You a Hitchcock fan or what?'

'Funny story,' he said. 'Last year Stuart Pearce scored a penalty for Nottingham Forest against Luton in the eighty-ninth minute. Alec Chamberlain was the goalie. Brought the score to two all. And it brought my score up to eight draws. I won half a million quid that afternoon. Bought this.' His gesture encompassed the building. 'I was that far away – ' he held his finger and thumb in front of himself about a quarter of an inch apart '– to losing the whole lot. Pearce's nickname's "Psycho". When I found out what he'd done, I named the house after him. Good, eh?'

'Marvellous,' I said. 'Good morning.' And left.

Just as well it wasn't 'Bite your legs' Norman Hunter who scored, I thought, as I walked down the drive.

At the third house, Trencher's Farm, I struck lucky. I got invited in for a beer, and for probably the umpteenth time Geoffrey Godbold told me his story. Geoffrey is married to Arabella. They have a son called Anthony, and a dog called Trollope. I'll leave you to draw your own conclusions from that. On the night of the 28th of March the previous year, Arabella had been giving Trollope (a Highland Terrier) his nightly constitutional. Once back on the close, she took Trollope off his lead so that he could do in private anything he was loath to do in front of his mistress. He ran between the front gates of Oakfield, and through the open front door. Arabella followed and found him lapping blood out of Sandra Kellerman's eye socket. The eye apparently was elsewhere.

Geoffrey told me the last part with some relish. 'She picked up the dog and ran back here as if the hounds of hell were after her. I called the police and ambulance and went over and had a shufti. Took my bloody Webley with me just in case.' He explained: 'I've been vice-chairman of the local gun club for years.'

A one-man Tet Offensive, I thought.

Geoffrey told me that he found the bodies and waited, gun in hand, for the law to arrive. 'They bloody nearly ran me in,' he said. 'First bloke on the scene almost shit his pants when he saw the side arm.'

I wasn't surprised. I think I might have needed a change of

underwear myself, turning up at that house on that night to find that gorehound standing in the passage waving a bloody great cannon around.

'Soon got it sorted out though,' said Geoffrey. 'Explained I'd never had any trouble with the neighbours.' He brayed a particularly unpleasant laugh, and I thanked him for his help and left my beer and the house.

That was it for Crown Point for me that day.

On the way home I checked the local newspaper office files on the story of the murder. I'd given up any idea of a kind policeman donating his. Robber had told me a bit in the pub when I'd met him – more than he'd probably meant to – but not enough. I wanted all the information I could get. The consensus was that it had been a professional killing. No one had been seen going in or out of the house. No clues were found. Nothing that was released to the papers anyway. No shotgun cartridges, no footprints, fingerprints, and the only strange tyre tracks that had been found were unidentified. Whoever killed the Kellermans had got in and out clean. Just like Robber had said.

I made a note to check that with Webb, amongst other things. Just to be sure.

But the first call I made when I got in was to Swansea. I had the number of the Ford that had followed me that morning. It's illegal to obtain information from the DVLC unless authorised, difficult too, but possible if you know the ways and means. I do. The licence number I had memorised was issued to the Metropolitan Police. How convenient. I telephoned Gipsy Hill Police and got through to Robber, the nosey bugger. 'Are you having me followed?'

'What if I am?'

'You want to get a better car or a better driver. What are they teaching these boys at Hendon these days?'

'Bollocks!' he said.

'Listen, you've only got to ask and I'll tell you where I'm going. I'll post an itinerary on the door every morning if you like.'

'I wanted to see if you'd take my advice.'

'And knock it on the head?'

'S'right.'

'Or maybe see if I stirred up anything that would do you a bit of good.'

'Don't take liberties, Sharman. And also, if you're seen driving like you were this morning again, I'll have you nicked. Now piss off, I'm busy.'

'Yes, Mr Robber,' I said. You'll have to catch me first, I thought, as I hung up.

Next I phoned James Webb. He confirmed the information I'd got from my meeting with Robber, and latterly from the newspaper files.

'Any news for me?' he asked.

'Well, I don't think this case is quite as dead as you seem to think.'

'Why?'

'I'm being followed.'

'Followed? Who by?'

'The police. Our mate Robber's stuck a car on my tail.'

'Why's that, do you think?'

'Your guess is as good as mine, but it's obvious the case isn't closed.'

'They haven't done much.'

'Maybe more than you know, Jim. He was certainly upset when I started putting my oar in.'

'So what do you think?'

'I don't like it,' I said. 'I'm having second thoughts. Second *bad* thoughts.'

There was a long pause before he spoke. 'I've paid you. I'm counting on your help.'

'Sure,' I said. 'But just for a week. Step softly, Jim. If you see or hear anything weird, call me.'

'I will.'

I asked him if the Kellermans had been buried or cremated. He told me they were buried in Streatham cemetery. I asked for the plot number. He asked me why I wanted it. I said I was going to visit the grave. He asked me why. I told him because it was there. It wasn't the most pleasant thing to say but it shut him up. I felt lousy about it after, but I was beginning to hate the case, and I was getting jumpy.

Finally I telephoned the BBC. Got through to the right person too. After twenty minutes of being transferred round the Television Centre, I spoke to a female researcher in the *Crimewatch UK* office. Her name was Norah. She sounded young. I gave her the full half hour. Who I was and what I was doing, and what I wanted. She talked to me although probably she shouldn't.

It transpired that, after the segment on the murders, only five calls were received. It was a very poor response. Every one turned out to be a hoax or malicious.

I thanked her, and she told me it was a pleasure and waited for me to ask her out, to tell her all about what I was doing. I let her wait. I had enough women problems as it was.

That was me for the day. I walked down to Norwood and had a Chinese. I hate eating on my own. Then I went to the bar and had a few beers. It was very crowded that night. So crowded, in fact, that if I sat very still I could pretend I was invisible.

7

The next morning I phoned Jim first thing. I apologised for cutting him off the previous day and tried to explain how I felt: jumpy, as if something bad was going to happen soon. Then he started apologising too. We both accepted each other's apologies and that was that.

Then I asked him for the address and number of Natalie Hooper, Kellerman's secretary, and the number of The Intercontinental Carpet Company's accountant. He gave me both. I told him I'd get back to him.

I stayed on the phone and tried the secretary. An answerphone cut in after the third ring. I left my name and number. Then I tried the accountant. His office was in Croydon and his name was Andrew Cunningham. He worked for a firm with a lot of names on the letterhead. His was last on the list, but at least it was there. He was in when I called, and told me he could spare me fifteen minutes at four-thirty that afternoon. He almost made me feel honoured. I made the appointment.

Then I telephoned a few people I knew. They were all in the business one way or another. All professed ignorance of the murders and all wondered why I was chasing the case at such a late date.

So did I.

Even when I offered cash incentives I got no takers. It was obvious that, if I wanted some information, I'd have to get my boogie shoes on.

So around lunchtime, I decided to make a tour of some of the boozers I know where the lads hang out. Or in police parlance, 'where known criminals consort'. It's got a lovely ring to it has that expression. You sort of expect spit and sawdust, striped jerseys and black sacks with SWAG stencilled on them. Don't you believe it! These days villains love their comforts as much as anyone. I was followed by a red Montego. I made a mental note of the licence plate, but didn't bother to try and lose the tail.

The first boozer I touched down at was a bit of Olde England down by the gasworks at Sydenham. The place groaned with false timbers and wrought iron. The missus groaned with false eyelashes and wrought twenty-four carat gold. I bought a bottle of Grolsch and we had a good old giggle together when I popped the china top.

'Does Stan McKilkenney still drink in here?' I asked her.

'You know Stan?'

'Like a brother.'

'Yes,' she said. 'I expect he'll be in in a minute.'

'Good,' I said. 'I'll wait.' It's amazing. I hadn't seen Stan in two or three years, but I knew if he wasn't banged up he'd be in that bar sometime during the lunch hour. It never ceases to amaze me how little people change their habits. I sat on a bar stool and looked at the menu chalked on a blackboard on the wall. I've never liked pub food. I had too much of it when I was in the job. It's always meant to be like your mother made. My mother is a chronic cook. Her gravy comes in slices and you can sole shoes with it. I was mentally tossing up between the delights of Lord Kitchener's steak and kidney pie and Mrs Bridges' special sausage, mash and onion when Stan McKilkenney chose that moment to come in and save my digestion.

He didn't see me and went straight to the bar. The missus spoke to him and just for a moment his expression slipped and I saw naked fear on his face. When you live like Stan lives, strange men of a certain age making enquiries about you behind pub bars often means Old Bill is looking for a convenient body to pull in for questioning. When he looked over to where I was sitting and recognised me he blew a sigh of relief and came over. I watched him as he crossed the carpet towards me. Stan was middle-aged and fighting a heavy rearguard action. He fancied himself as something of a dandy, but take my word he was never going to get into Britain's ten best dressed. He had an unfortunate and enduring faith in man-made fibres. And I swear he was colour blind.

That day he was wearing a coffee-coloured pork pie hat tilted forward over one eye. His grey hair had been Grecian 2000'd into yellow streaks and he had sideburns Elvis would have envied before he went into the army. His shirt was bottle green and unbuttoned halfway to his waist. The long points of the collar were artfully arranged outside the lapels of a pale blue suit with a waisted jacket, and a subtle flare at the ankles of the trousers. On his feet he wore fake white Gucci shoes with tarnished gold chains across the tops. There was an equally tarnished gold chain nestling in his grey chest hair. He was a sartorial disaster. He even made the pub grub look attractive.

'Nick Sharman,' he said when he got up close. 'Well, I'll be buggered.'

'Stan the man,' I said, picking a piece of lint from the shoulder of his jacket. 'You looked a bit worried there, my son. Who were you expecting? The forces of law and order?'

'No. I'm clean these days, Nick.'

'Seems to me I've heard that song somewhere before, Stan.'

'It's true. As I live and breathe.'

'I believe you,' I said. 'I always used to, didn't I?'

'You did.'

'You mugged me off rotten.'

'You were always fair, Nick.'

'That's not what my guv'nors used to say.'

'It's all part of the ebb and flow of life.'

'Philosophy, Stan. I love it.'

'I went to the Greek Islands last year,' he said. 'You'd be amazed what I learned. I bought a book.'

'Christ, Stan, that's a first.'

'No, Nick, I'm a great reader.'

'Sauce bottles?'

'No, books.'

'Picked it up inside, did you?'

'I was librarian last time,' he said proudly.

'Great career move, Stan. I'm proud of you.'

'So what can I do for you?'

'Information, Stan. Pure and simple.'

'How much?' He rubbed a finger and thumb together. I told you he never changed.

'For free. To pay back for some of those times I believed you, when maybe a more diligent officer would have dug deeper.'

'That's history, Nick.'

'Give me a break, Stan. I've given you more than your fair share in my time.'

'What about a drink then?'

'Vera?' I asked.

'Double.'

I called over the missus and ordered him a large gin and tonic and waited for her to leave before continuing: 'So what's occurring?'

'Seems like I should ask you that. What do you want to know about?'

'Kellerman. Know the name?'

He shook his head.

'A whole family murdered in Crown Point. Shot. Big house. He was in the carpet trade.'

'I'm not.'

'Do me a favour, Stan. Do you remember the case?'

'Vaguely.'

'Know anything about it?'

'Fuck off, Nick.' He almost choked on his gin. 'When did I ever use violence?'

'Not you yourself, you prat,' I said. 'Have you heard a whisper?'

'It was fucking years ago.'

'Fifteen months or so,' I said. He took another long swallow of his drink. 'Another?' I asked.

'Wouldn't say no.'

I'd never known him to before. I got in another beer for me and a reprise of the gin.

'Heavy duty,' he said.

'That's a fact,' I agreed. 'Any ideas?'

'I don't know…'

'Come on, Stan,' I said. 'You know everything that goes off around here.'

'Well…' he said. But he did, and we both knew it. 'Why are you interested?'

'Professional. The brother of Mrs Kellerman has no faith in the judiciary.'

'It's a crime, isn't it?' he said. Witty too. Razor sharp. 'What would it be worth?'

I knew we'd get round to that subject again sooner or later. He wasn't backward in coming forward, our Stanley. Did you really expect I'd get anything out of him for the price of a couple of gins? 'The geezer's not short,' I said. 'And he's prepared to pay. But not for anything snide.'

'As if!'

'Stan, don't mug me off again.'

'No, straight, Nick. I'll ask around. But it has to be worth a monkey.'

'For you to ask around? Do me a favour. I don't get paid that sort of money.'

'For hard information?'

'Now that is possible.'

'Something out front?'

'A tenner?'

'A tenner doesn't buy a round in here these days.'

'Maybe you should stick to lemonade.'

'What, with my image to keep up?'

I really didn't want to get on to the subject of his image at that point. 'Fifty,' I said.

'That'll do nicely.'

I took out five tens in a little bundle I'd prepared earlier. I knew to the penny what Stan thought he was worth. And that included inflation. He palmed the notes without interrupting his conversational flow. 'Thanks,' he said. 'I'm glad you dropped by today.'

'I just bet you are. How long will this asking around take?'

'A day or two.'

'Make it tomorrow.'

'That might be a bit soonish.'

'And what else are you doing that's so urgent?' I enquired.

'This and that. I've got a living to earn, you know.'

'Drawing the dole and spending it in Joe Coral's. Do me a favour, Stan. Get off your tuckus and earn the dough.'

'I'm a busy man, Nick. Honest.'

'That's two porky pies in one breath, son. Tomorrow.'

'All right. Just for you I'll put everything else on the back burner.'

The only thing on his back burner was his old woman's chip pan, but I let it go. 'I'm obliged, Stan,' I said. And finished my beer. He looked sadly into his empty glass but I wasn't going to stay and buy him drinks all afternoon. 'Same time tomorrow, then.'

'I'll be here.'

I knew that I could count on that. The only problem was

getting him to leave the place in the meantime. 'See you then,' I said.

'See you.'

I slipped off my stool and left. I went back to my car and drove towards Dulwich. There was a little boozer on the other side of the village I wanted to visit. The red Montego was nowhere to be seen. I guessed that they'd gone off duty or got a call about something really important. I got to the second pub just after two. This one had recently been converted into a 1930s speakeasy or somesuch. Personally I'd rather have an ordinary drinker and cheaper beer. But what do I know? As I hadn't eaten earlier I risked a cheese and pickle sandwich with my Corona and slice of lime.

I'd hardly taken two bites when the landlord came over. 'I thought I recognised that beast parked outside,' he said, and stuck out his hand. I put down the remains of my sandwich, wiped my hand on my jeans and took it. 'Terry,' I said.

'How are you, Nick?'

'Not as good as you are by the looks of it.'

Terry Mayhew had been a copper too. A straight one. One of the few I'd got on with. God knows why, we couldn't have been more different. But they do say that opposites attract. He'd done twenty-five years' service, the last eight as a uniformed sergeant. Then retirement and a nice pension. He was something big in the Masons, and he'd been taken on by a brewery to sort out a couple of hard pubs that were spoiling their image. No problem there. Terry was six foot four and fifteen stone. An ex-player for the Metropolitan Police rugby team who didn't know the meaning of the word fear. He'd sorted out both difficult boozers within six months, then a few more over the years, and as a reward had been given this place.

He was looking good as it happened. His blue worsted suit was tailor made – it needed to be with the size of his chest – and if I wasn't mistaken his cream shirt was pure silk. I'd've laid even money it was monogrammed.

'It's been a while,' he said. 'I read about you in the papers.'

'You don't believe everything you read in them, do you?'

He laughed and got me a vodka and orange juice. 'On the house, mate,' he said. 'What *does* bring you here?'

'To see how the other half lives,' I said.

'I was lucky, Nick.'

'That's not what I heard. You keeping up with the local gossip?'

'Depends.'

'Come on, Terry,' I said. 'This is the tidiest bar in the area. I've heard all about it. The villains love drinking in here. No trouble.'

'I try and keep it clean.'

'Which is exactly why you might hear things. They trust you, Terry.'

'So you're working?'

'Sure. For a bloke called Webb.' I went through the story again. Terry knew what I was talking about. He obviously kept up. It's a habit you get into.

'I've never heard a word about it in here,' he said. 'It sounds like a rough one.'

'When did that ever bother you?'

'I'm slowing down, Nick. I'll be fifty next year.'

'On you it looks good.'

'Clean living.'

I laughed. 'How *is* the wife?' Her name was Annie. A real smasher. She worshipped the ground he walked on, and the feeling was mutual.

'Out spending the profits. Come by and see her soon. She always had a soft spot for you.'

'It's my magical charm,' I said. 'Course I will.' I should have long ago, but it was difficult. They both reminded me of a different time. A different place. When anything seemed possible.

'Anytime. She'll be sorry she missed you. And I'm sorry I can't help with the other thing.'

'Well, if you do hear of anything, Terry.'

'You'll be the first to know. But it's well out of date.'

'That's what everybody says,' I replied. 'But someone, somewhere, knows something.'

He looked into the distance thoughtfully. 'I'll tell you what I'll do… there's a couple of people I could, you know, discreetly enquire of.'

'I'd be grateful,' I said. 'Here's my home number.' I scribbled it down on the back of one of my business cards. Terry tucked it away in his wallet.

'Want to stay for a drink?' he asked.

'With you? Are you kidding. I've been caught like that before. Anyway, I'm driving. Another time.'

'Make it soon. Don't be such a stranger.'

'I will,' I said. 'Give my best to Annie.' I finished the vodka and drove home. Once again no one followed.

8

I kicked my heels around at my flat until it was time to go and visit the accountant.

Andrew Cunningham had a pleasant office in an unpleasant glass block looking over the motorway that cuts Croydon in half. I used the car park underneath and paid for the privilege. They'll tow you away in a second down there.

Cunningham's secretary showed me in. He stood up behind his desk to shake hands and waved me to the client's chair. He was of average height, slim, with brown hair neatly combed, wearing an anonymous grey suit, white shirt and a striped tie. He looked like exactly what he was.

I explained again why I was there. By that time I was after the sympathy vote.

He made a steeple of his hands as he listened. His fingernails were clean and clipped very short. I guessed he was thirty-five or six going on sixty. After he'd listened, he said: 'Although Mr Kellerman is dead, any business dealings he had with us are still confidential.'

'His brother-in-law has hired me to look into the matter of his death,' I told him for the third time.

'Mr Webb found it convenient not to use our services after Mr Kellerman's unfortunate demise,' said Cunningham. 'Demise'. He really said that. I wished I'd brought the photos to show him. They'd give him 'demise'. 'So I can't speculate on any financial matters after that date.'

So that was it, professional jealousy.

'The business was going bust,' I said.

He nodded.

'Did you expect that to happen?'

'It shouldn't have. Not so quickly. But, of course, when the founder and chief executive dies under such appalling circumstances, the accounts will obviously come under close scrutiny. Large financial organisations, or even for that matter small, are apt to be rather jittery. Especially these days.' He said it as if he expected the Four Horsemen of the Apocalypse to come round the one-way system at any moment. 'I'm afraid it was inevitable. I understand Mr Webb put it into receivership almost immediately.'

I nodded. 'But it would have happened eventually?'

He looked at me across his empty, polished desk. 'Mr Sharman,' he said, 'I liked David Kellerman. I was sorry–' He grimaced and seemed more human and younger. 'Sorry is hardly the word. I was devastated at what happened. I knew the family. Sandra was a wonderful woman. But – and I shouldn't be telling you this, and will deny it if anyone ever asks – there was too much money in the business for a long time, and then there was too little.'

'When was there too little?'

'About three months before he died. Around Christmas the previous year. That's when it began to show.'

'Did he do the books or did you?'

'He did. He was very particular about that. David was something of a genius with figures.'

I just bet he was, I thought. 'Then why employ you?'

'It's the law. The Companies Act, you know.' I didn't. 'But I just acted as an overseer. I checked that everything was all right at audit time. I wasn't just employed for my accountancy skills – David and I were friends. Any halfway decent firm could have done the job. We went out for drinks. Lunch. I think a lot of the time I was someone to talk to.'

I looked at my watch. My fifteen minutes was nearly up, so I jumped in at the deep end. 'Was he laundering money?' I asked.

Cunningham was silent for a moment. He looked at me closely. 'I told you, he was a friend,' he said. 'Now he's dead I don't intend to slander his name. If he was doing anything illegal, he didn't confide in me. This is an honest firm, Mr Sharman. Honestly run. Perhaps I should have dug a little deeper. But as I said, we were friends. I hope that by not doing so I didn't encourage any act that put David and his family in danger. I'd find that very difficult to live with. I hope you find the people who did it. Now I'm afraid I have another appointment,' he said. He buzzed for his secretary and she showed me out.

I went home and tried Natalie Hooper's number again. Again the machine. Again the message.

I didn't fancy going out. I cooked a meal out of tins and sat and watched TV without seeing a thing. Cat sidled up and sat on me.

I drank a couple of bottles of beer and smoked another joint and went to bed when the late film finished around twelve-fifteen.

9

That night I dreamt of my old friend Wanda. Wanda the Cat Woman, I called her. We've been friends for years. She's looked after my cat several times when I've been otherwise engaged: on a case, in hospital or in the nick. I hadn't seen her for months, not since I got Cat back the last time.

It had been a bad dream. A real doozy. Not one after which you could just turn over in your warm bed and go back to sleep and be grateful it was only a dream.

No, this was a classic, a black, fearful nightmare, and I woke, sitting up with a scream in my throat and the sheets tangled and wet with sweat around my legs. I was shaking from head to toe. I scrambled for cigarettes and matches. The smoke tasted foul in my mouth.

There's nothing more tedious than other people's dreams, I know, but this one – boy, it freaked me right out.

I was in Wanda's house, but of course it wasn't hers, only in the dream it was. She hated me, in the dream. Detested me. And told me so. She listed every lousy thing I was and that I'd done. Even things she couldn't possibly have known about. I tried to justify myself, but it was no good. I knew she was right, see.

The dream seemed to last for ever, and she kept on and on. I told her all about the honourable and decent things I'd done in my life, and she turned them round until they seemed like nothing.

The next morning I still remembered the dream, and feeling guilty about not having been in touch for so long, I phoned her.

'Hello, Nick,' she said when she answered the phone and I identified myself. She sounded tired. 'It's been a while.'

'Yeah,' I said. 'Sorry.'

'I suppose you want something?'

I remembered the dream and winced. 'No,' I said. 'I just wondered how you were.'

She laughed, and the laugh turned into a cough. 'I'm fine,' she said, but the way she said it I knew she wasn't, and I went cold and sweaty all over again.

'What's up?' I asked.

'Who knows?'

'Wanda,' I said, 'what is it? Tell me.'

'You just caught me actually. I'm going into hospital.'

I knew by her voice, but I asked anyway. 'Bad?'

'Is going into hospital ever good?'

'There are degrees.'

'Yes, there are,' she said, and left me to ask again.

'Come on, Wanda,' I said. 'Tell me. On a scale of one to ten.'

'Nine.'

'Shit.'

'Yes, it is, Nick, but really I'm tired of talking about it. I've got to go now, there's a taxi coming.' And she hung up.

I called back but the answerphone was on. She hadn't even told me what hospital she was going into. There aren't that many around any more and I could have telephoned around the few that were left, but it was obvious she didn't want me to.

I fed Cat and made myself a brew of coffee. Black and bitter, just the way I felt myself. I knew my premonition had been right.

I knew that something terrible was going to happen. I felt like Cunningham in his steel and glass tower waiting for the Four Horsemen to come.

Right then I didn't know the half of it.

10

10

I was back in the pub at Sydenham for lunchtime. The missus didn't look so hot that day. Or so friendly. I went up to the bar to order a drink, and she was pointing at me before I could get a word out. I turned and two men were standing behind me and sticking their warrant cards in my face.

'Detective Sergeant Williams,' said the taller of the two. He was blond, wearing a trench coat like Dick Tracy's. 'And this is my colleague, Detective Constable Hackett.' I looked at the other one. He was shorter, dark, wearing a bomber jacket, jeans and trainers.

I knew something bad was up, but I decided to brazen it out. 'Nice,' I said. 'Can I get a beer now?'

'I don't think so,' said Hackett. 'Were you in here yesterday?'

'That's right,' I said.

'In the company of Stanley McKilkenney?'

'Right again. I'm supposed to be meeting him in here again today.'

'I don't think so,' said Williams.

'Why? Have you nicked him again?' I asked.

'Not quite.' Williams again.

'What then?'

'You haven't been listening to the news this morning.'

Then I knew that something *big* and bad was up. 'No,' I said.

'Stanley McKilkenny was found early this morning in the boot of a car – dead,' said Williams. 'Someone had put a double-barrelled shotgun in his mouth and pulled both triggers. His head had gone. He was only identified by his fingerprints.'

'And his suit,' said Hackett, who seemed to be enjoying the whole thing immensely. The missus heard the last bit and ran out of the bar holding a handkerchief to her eyes. 'So you can't get a beer, but you can come with us down to the station to answer a few questions.'

'Why?' I asked. 'I didn't shoot him.' But I had a bloody good idea who did. Poor old Stan, he never hurt a fly in his life. The poor sod didn't deserve that kind of death. Nobody did.

'To help us with our enquiries. You were one of the last people to see him alive,' said Hackett.

'But not *the* last.'

'That's for us to discover,' said Williams.

I shook my head sadly. 'You're barking up the wrong tree here, officers,' I said. 'But if you insist.'

'We do,' said Williams.

'Let's go then.'

We went outside to a regulation navy blue Vauxhall Cavalier that smelt of stale cigarettes and carry-out food. It quite took me back. We drove to Sydenham police station where I was taken down to an interview room by Williams. It was real nice. No windows. A twin deck cassette recorder. A metal table bolted to the floor, and three plastic chairs. A panic strip ran round all four walls. A uniformed constable came with us. I was in the chair opposite the door. Hackett came in a few minutes later with two sealed C90 cassettes. It looked like they were expecting a long afternoon. Williams told the uniform to wait outside.

'May I smoke?' I asked, after he'd gone.

'If you must.' Williams.

'Do you want to call your solicitor?' Hackett.

'I haven't done anything. I'll be out before he gets here,' I said.

'Don't you believe it.' Hackett again. He really didn't like me. And it hurt.

I lit a Silk Cut. I only had four left.

'You know all about this, don't you?' said Williams, holding up the two cassettes Hackett had given him.

'Yes,' I said.

'He knows about everything,' said Hackett spitefully. 'And we know all about him.'

'Is that right?' I asked.

'That's right,' said Hackett. 'And you're going to go down.'

'And you're going to take me down, are you?'

'Maybe.'

'Maybe,' I said. 'But not today.'

'Are you two finished?' asked Williams.

'I am,' I said. 'I don't know about Judge Dredd, the one-man army here.'

Hackett said nothing, but he was white with fury.

'Good,' said Williams. 'Then let's get on.' He put both cassettes in the machine, pushed the 'Record' button, reeled off the time and date, those present and what the interview concerned. At last I was going to make a record. He sat down opposite me.

'Mr Sharman,' he said, 'why did you go and see Stanley McKilkenney yesterday afternoon?'

'I was just looking up an old acquaintance,' I said.

'Christ!' interrupted Hackett. 'We'll be singing *Auld Lang Syne* in a minute.' Williams gave him a dirty look.

'How long since you've seen him?' asked Williams.

'A long time. Two years at least. Maybe three.'

'And why yesterday?'

'Spur-of-the-moment thing. You know how it is.'

'So you've not been in regular communication?'

'We don't send Christmas cards, if that's what you mean.'

'No, that's not what I mean at all. What I mean is, you haven't been seeing him on a regular basis?'

'I already said that.'

'So can you tell me what transpired at the meeting yesterday?' I must say he was beautifully spoken.

'I bought him a couple of drinks. We talked about old times. I left.'

'The landlady at the pub overheard you saying you'd see him again today.'

'I already told you that. That's why I was there.'

'So suddenly, after a three-year gap, you decide to get together again after just twenty-four hours?'

'He's an attractive bloke,' I said. I was starting to get pissed off, and thinking that maybe refusing a solicitor wasn't such a good idea after all.

'Come along, Mr Sharman,' said Williams. 'He was hardly your type. You drive an E-Type and wear Armani suits. He had a bus pass and shopped at Oxfam.'

'It takes all sorts.'

'So what were you – soul mates?' Hackett.

'Something like that.'

'And you didn't see him later last night?' Williams.

'No.'

'So where exactly were you? Say between the hours of 10 pm last night and 2 am this morning?'

'At home. I watched TV. Went to bed at twelve or a bit after.'

'Alone?'

'My morals are spotless,' I said, although I was finding it harder and harder to find any levity in the conversation.

'So you can't prove it?' Hackett.

'Do I have to? I've known Stan for a long time. He wasn't what I'd call a great friend, but he was harmless. I had no reason to kill him. I liked the poor little sod. Now why don't you two get the fuck out on to the streets and find out who did?'

'Tea, I think,' said Williams, and gave the time and reason for interrupting the interview, and turned off the tape machine.

'Now the fun begins, I suppose,' I said.

'No,' said Williams. 'Unless you consider station tea to be fun. Pete, will you?' he said to Hackett. 'I think I'll be safe with Mr Sharman.'

Hackett left and I lit another cigarette. Things were getting serious. Perhaps it was time to give a bit. 'Did Stan have any money on him when you found him?' I asked.

'Like?' said Williams.

'Like five tenners wrapped up together.'

He took them out of his pocket and threw them on the table in front of me. 'Now how did you know that?' he asked.

'I gave them to him yesterday. And before you start, I didn't go and try and get them back last night at the point of a gun.'

'Why did you give them to him?'

'He used to snout for me. Not high profile, just a bit of info here and there. I'm working on a case now. A murder. Last year. Local. Up at Crown Point. I asked him to sniff about for me. That was the down payment.' I pointed to the money.

'What murder?'

'The Kellermans.'

He nodded. 'Who are you working for?'

'James Webb. Sandra Kellerman's brother.'

He looked at the wall. I didn't know what he was thinking.

'Straight,' I said. 'Ask Robber.'

He looked back at me. 'Jack Robber?'

'That's right. I went and saw him the other night. He's had me followed for the last couple of days. They were with me when I went to the pub yesterday. They must have seen who I met. I'm hardly likely to go off and murder the poor bleeder after that, am I?'

'Followed?' he said, like he didn't believe me. 'By whom?' I told you he spoke well.

'Robber's firm, I suppose. An Escort on Tuesday. A Montego yesterday.'

'What colour Montego?' He was suddenly very interested. Too interested. But it was too late to stop by then.

'Red,' I said.

'Did you get the number?'

'Christ, it wasn't... ?' I said.

'Did you?'

I reeled it off from memory. I saw his fists clench. 'It was, wasn't it?' I said.

'Yes,' he said. 'That was the car McKilkenny was found in. I think I'd better go and speak to Jack Robber.'

I felt like I'd been punched in the stomach. Williams got up and went to the door and called the uniform back in and left us. I lit another cigarette. I sat, and the uniform stood, and we looked at each other. I remember doing that job myself, long ago. I always hated it. You're not supposed to speak, see.

Five minutes later Hackett came in with tea and KitKats. If it hadn't been so serious I would have laughed. KitKats, I ask you. Hackett sat down and ate his chocolate and drank his tea and didn't say a word. That made three dummies in the room.

Williams came back about twenty minutes later. He dismissed the uniform before he spoke. He didn't put the tape recorder back on. 'I've spoken to Detective Inspector Robber,' he said. 'You were followed for one day. Or part of it. Apparently you lost them. It was the Escort. He knows nothing about a Montego.'

'So?' I said.

'So you can go. It looks like the Kellerman case is active again. Take my advice and stop working on it, as of now.'

'Unless, of course, Stan was into something else,' I said. But it was a slim chance.

'I doubt it,' said Williams. 'He's been on these streets for over fifty years, apart from when he's been inside. The worst that's happened to him was a broken ankle a couple of years ago. Then you come along and get him involved in something and he's dead within twenty-four hours. You were right, Stan was a decent bloke as villains go. You've already got a lot to live with, Sharman. Now there's one more on your conscience. I wonder how you manage to sleep at nights.'

I didn't bother telling him that most nights I didn't. Or that when I did, how the nightmares haunted me. I don't think I'd have got much sympathy. None in fact.

'Do you want your fifty quid back?' he asked sarcastically.

'No,' I said. 'Maybe his wife…'

'I'll make sure she gets it,' he said. 'I expect Jack Robber will be round to see you. And, Sharman, if he's not, *I* will be. You haven't heard the last of this.'

Hackett saw me off the premises. He didn't say a word. I walked back to the pub, picked up my car and drove home.

Slowly.

11

When I got back to my flat, I phoned Webb and told him what had happened.

'I don't believe it,' he said.

'It's true.'

'And they really thought that you did it?'

'I don't think so. It was convenient. I was there. But if it had anything to do with me asking him to help, then I'm responsible.'

'And me.'

'No, I involved him.'

'Do you think it was to do with Sandy's murder?'

'Probably.'

'Do you think he found anything out?'

'We'll never know now. Maybe it was a warning.'

'A warning?'

'To me. To get lost.'

'And?'

'The police warned me off too. They're looking for Stan's killer or killers now. They'll look into any connection between his murder and the murder of your sister's family. The case is live again. That's what you wanted, isn't it?'

He was silent for a moment. 'So you're quitting?'

'That's right.'

'You really are scared.'

What the fuck did he know? 'Like I told you, every day of my life. If you want your money back…'

'No, keep it.'

'Thanks a bunch,' I said. 'Listen, Jim, I'll catch up with you another day. I'll get the keys of Oakfield back to you.'

'There's no rush.'

'And take it easy, Jim. There's at least one mad bastard still out there. Five people are dead. So watch yourself.'

'And you.'

'I'm an expert.'

'Bye, then.'

'Bye,' I said, and hung up the phone.

But it wasn't quite over for me yet. I took out the photo of the Kellermans that James Webb had given me, and I looked at it hard and long. Then I got into the car and drove to the cemetery. I found the grave easily. I read the inscription on the collective tombstone. It didn't say much. The grave was neat and well tended. I bought a cheap bunch of flowers at the stall at the entrance to the cemetery and arranged them in one of the pots at the corner of the plot.

I was glad to be off the case. It had been a fuck up from the beginning. I looked at the photo again as I stood there, then I went home.

That night I got drunk alone. I drank toasts to Stan and Wanda and the Kellermans. When I finally slept I dreamt of them all. They were by the pool in the photo. They were having fun but I knew it couldn't last. Something unspeakable was coming that would end in blood and pain. I tried to warn them but they wouldn't listen. I screamed and screamed at them until I woke myself up, and I still don't know to this day if I was screaming out loud.

I didn't sleep again that night.

The next morning I went to the bank and took out the thousand quid in cash that Webb had paid me and took it round to Stan McKilkenney's flat. He and his wife had lived in the same council block in Sydenham since I'd known him. Thank Christ she wasn't there. I didn't want to face her. Their married daughter was. I gave her the money. She told me that her mum was at the undertakers. I didn't leave a name. I wanted Mrs McKilkenney to keep the money, not burn it. I said I was an old friend.

Some friend.

I went back home and got drunk again. I tried to stay that way all weekend.

12

By Sunday I was so well into a three-day drunk that I was down to the cooking sherry and out of cigarettes and Cat had temporarily left home and taken up residence with the Indian family who lived four doors down and fed him leftover chicken tandoori and lamb tikka. At twelve I went to the off-licence for supplies. Just as well. In the afternoon Detective Inspector Robber came to call.

Apparently he'd been ringing the bell for more than five minutes when the people in the ground floor flat took pity on him and let him in. When he knocked on my flat door I thought it was one of the neighbours inviting me to an 'At home' with wine and quiche and Chris Rea on the CD player. He was lucky I answered at all.

'Are you deaf?' he asked when I finally opened the door.

'No,' I said. 'Come in and have a drink.' After three solitary days with only a succession of bottles for company, even Robber was welcome.

He did as I asked and sat in the only armchair and looked around the room. 'This place is a tip.'

'The cleaning lady took umbrage with my lifestyle. Beer,

Scotch, vodka – what do you want?'

'Scotch,' he said.

'Ice?'

'Water.'

I made him a drink, gave it to him, then poured one for myself and perched on the kitchen stool. I was so drunk that the air in the room felt like Vaseline and I had a nagging ache behind my eyes that made me squint. 'So what's new, Inspector?' I asked and lit a cigarette. My fingers were shaking so much I had to hold the match with both hands.

He didn't answer. 'What's all this about then? Feeling a bit sorry for yourself?' His voice sounded like it was coming out of a tube tunnel.

'And others,' I said.

'Bollocks! You haven't got it in you.'

'Is this a social call?' I asked. 'Because if it is, and that's all you can say, you can fuck right off.'

'You going to make me?'

At that moment I don't think I could have got myself out of the flat, let alone him. 'No,' I said, and took a swallow of my drink and spilled some down my chin and shirt front. See what I mean? 'Have you got anyone for Stan's murder yet?'

'I wondered when you'd ask. No, not yet.'

'Another triumph for our boys in blue.'

'You really are a prick, aren't you?'

'I think the jury's still out on that one,' I replied.

'Not from where I'm sitting.'

'OK, Mr Robber. Now the pleasantries are out of the way, what do you want?'

'What do you think, Sharman? A man was murdered last week. You were one of the last to see him alive. You gave him money to ask around on your behalf. I want to know what you know.'

'Didn't Williams fill you in?'

'Some. But you tell me.'

'Is this your case now?'

'If it has anything to do with the Kellerman murders, it's my case.'

So I told him. Everything I knew. It was precious little. When I'd finished, he said: 'And you've stopped working for James Webb?'

'Wouldn't you?'

He shrugged. 'But *I'm* not you,' he said.

Thank God, I thought. 'Do you think the person or persons who killed Stan are the same ones who killed the Kellermans?' I asked.

He nodded.

'The car you found Stan in – was it stolen or what?'

He nodded. 'That morning. From Penge railway station.'

'Did you find anything in it?'

'Only him.'

Funny, I thought.

'You should have phoned in about it following you,' he said.

'I phoned in about the other one and got a flea in my ear, as I remember. Maybe you should have kept a tail on me a bit longer.'

But there was really no point in 'ifs' and 'buts'.

'And I let them follow me,' I said. 'Shit! I could have lost them easily too.'

We sat in silence again. 'So I might be next?' I said eventually.

'I'm surprised they haven't done for you already.'

'Nice of you to say so.'

He shrugged again. I was just another bright spot in his day. Through the haze of booze I was starting to get his drift. 'You want me to carry on, don't you?'

'Christ, but you're quick.'

'Like a Judas goat?'

'You're already in the frame, son. I reckon the only reason you're walking about is because they don't know how many friends you've got.'

'And how many is that?'

'I could be one if you let me.'

'Christ, we'll be engaged next.'

He grinned. It wasn't a pretty sight. 'So?' he asked.

'I'll think about it.'

'Don't take too long. Cartridges are cheap.'

'How reassuring. Want another drink?' I did.

'Just the one,' he said.

'Late for lunch?'

'No. Pizza Hut stays open especially for me.'

'Not married?'

'Not in this job.'

Not in this world, I thought, looking at him. I poured a couple more drinks and lit another cigarette. The house and street were Sunday quiet. Someone far off was using a power mower. It was a far cry from talk of shotguns and murder. We drank our drinks in silence. When he finished his, he left. I was suddenly sober and missed having someone around for company. The phone rang. It was Mayhew. Even his cheery voice couldn't help.

'I've drawn a blank on what you asked, Nick. Sorry, mate, no one knows a thing.'

'It's OK, Terry, I'm not interested anyway. I'm off the case – it's got too serious for me.'

'That doesn't sound like you.'

'Yeah, well, it was one of my New Year's resolutions to stay alive.'

'Come and tell me about it.'

'Thanks, Terry, I might just do that.'

But I didn't. I poured another drink and switched on the TV. As I sat in the chair Robber'd vacated and sipped at my vodka, I thought about what he had said.

I sat there for the rest of the day, just thinking and drinking.

It was something to do.

13

On Monday morning I woke up with the mother of all hangovers. My head felt like it was made of glass and full of nitroglycerine just ready to explode. Cat came back from his travels, with the milk, and I was feeding him when the telephone rang.

'Mr Sharman?' a female voice asked.

'Yes.'

'Mr Nicholas Sharman.'

'Yes.'

'This is Sister Mackay here.'

'Yes?' I said, but I knew.

'From Princess Margaret Ward at St Thomas's Hospital.'

'Yes,' I said again.

'It's about Mrs Wanda Rice.'

'Yes.'

There was a pause. 'You are down as next of kin, you know, Mr Sharman.'

'Am I?'

'Well, don't you know?'

'I'm sorry, I don't,' I said. 'What's happened?'

'Don't you know that either?'

'No.'

The Sister sounded annoyed at my ignorance. 'Mrs Rice came in last Thursday for an operation. You do know that?'

'Yes,' I said.

'The operation was not a success. She knew the risks, and without it...' She didn't finish her sentence.

'Is she...' I didn't finish my sentence either.

She guessed what I was asking. How many other people hadn't finished that sentence in her career? I wondered. 'No, but the prognosis is not good.'

'Can I see her?'

'Of course. That's why I'm telephoning. She's asking to see you.'

'When?'

'Whenever you want. There are no visiting hours in these circumstances.'

'Now?'

'Yes. The sooner the better, I feel.'

'Will she recognise me?'

'She hasn't lost her mind, Mr Sharman.'

'I'm sorry. She didn't tell me anything about it, you see. It was pure coincidence that I got in touch with her last week.'

'I see.' But I'm sure she didn't.

'I'll be there in thirty minutes.'

'Good. I'll tell her.'

'Is she going to die?' I asked her. I sounded like a kid. Thank God she didn't make some smart reply. I couldn't have handled that. In fact, her tone softened.

'I'm afraid she is.'

'How long?'

'I don't know. But soon, very soon.'

'I'm on my way,' I said, and put the phone down and went and threw up. It made me feel better, but not much.

I dressed quickly and raced Cat to the front door. I broke the speed limit to Waterloo. The ward was on the top floor of the tower block at Tommy's. Wanda was in a small private room. The curtains were open and I looked down and saw the sun reflected on the surface of the river. Wanda was in bed with tubes coming out of her nose and mouth. She was wired into a machine that bleeped discreetly and more tubes were plugged into each arm. All the flesh had gone from her face and her skin was the same colour as the sheets and her eyes were closed. She was wearing a scarf turban-style around her head.

'Wanda,' I said. My voice sounded thick and too loud. She opened her eyes.

'Nick, I'm glad you're here.'

'Why didn't you tell me?'

'What could you have done?'

'Something, surely?'

'I doubt it.'

There was a straight-backed chair by the window. I pulled it close to the bed and sat down and touched her hand.

'Don't look at me,' she said. 'I must look awful.'

She did.

'No.'

'I haven't looked in a mirror for ages,' she said. 'I was looking so old and my hair started to fall out.' She pulled up the scarf and I saw that her hair, once so thick and shiny, was lying thin and lank and damp on her scalp. Seeing her there, nothing like the woman I'd once known, I realised that I didn't care what she looked like – I just felt sad that I was with possibly the best friend I had in the world, and she hadn't even told me she was sick. She probably thought that I couldn't have cared less. I held her hand. 'You're beautiful,' I said, and meant every word.

'Thank you, Nick. I'm grateful even if I know it's not true.'

I squeezed her hand gently. 'Yes, it is.'

She shook her head.

'I don't even know what's wrong with you,' I said.

'You're not much of a detective. Didn't you ask the nurse?'

I shook my head. 'I came straight in here.'

'I got a pain,' she said. 'A bad pain. Months ago. It wouldn't go away, so I went to the doctor. He sent me here. They told me I had cancer. They cut off my breasts.'

She started to cry. 'Anyway, apparently they found a lot more of the same. All over. Every bloody where they looked. The operation was a waste of time. I wish they'd just left me whole to die in peace…'

'I'm sorry. I didn't know…'

'Don't be embarrassed, Nick. You don't have to be embarrassed.'

'I'm sorry.'

'And don't be sorry.'

'For Christ's sake, let me be something!'

'That's better. That's more like the Nick I know.'

'And who's the Nick you know exactly?'

'That's right, Nick. Let's talk about you.'

'I'm sorry.'

'There you go again.'

'I don't know what to say.'

'*I'm* sorry, Nick. I shouldn't take it out on you. It's not your fault.'

'Don't be,' I said.

She smiled and for the first time she was the Wanda I recognised. 'Yeah, you're right,' she said. 'How's your girlfriend?'

'She's fine.' There was no point in going into details.

'That's good. Are you happy?'

'Who knows?'

'I am.'

I looked at her.

'You don't believe me?'

'Sure,' I said.

'No, you don't. But I am. At least I know what's in the future. Most people don't.'

'What's in the future is you out of here, and us going out for a drink.'

It was the wrong thing to say.

'No, Nick,' she said softly. 'No getting out, not for me.'

I started to argue but she shook her head. 'You don't have to pretend,' she said. 'Although I'm grateful for that too. I must be going soft in my old age.'

'What did you do with all those bloody cats?' I asked, changing the subject.

'They're all right. I found every one a home before I came in here.'

Typical Wanda. Always thinking of someone or something else first.

She asked me if I was working. I told her I had been. She asked me about the case. I think she just wanted to take her mind off her pain. I told her a bit about the Kellermans. Not a lot. Not even as much as I'd told Fiona at the Thai restaurant. Then I told her I'd knocked the enquiry on the head. I didn't tell her all the reasons.

'You didn't look very hard, did you?' she said.

I shrugged. What the hell, I thought.

'Those poor children,' she said. 'They didn't deserve to die. No matter what anyone had done, it wasn't their fault. You were their last chance.'

'Last chance for what?'

'Last chance for peace.'

'Jesus Christ, Wanda!' I said. 'Don't say that.'

'It's true.'

'Maybe it is.'

'You shouldn't give up, Nick. Life's too short.'

Maybe she was right. Maybe she wasn't. She lay back and her eyelids fluttered and she was asleep.

I sat with her for the rest of the day. She dozed and woke and we talked. About nothing mostly. Just after four I had to go and take a piss and smoke a cigarette. She was asleep. I gently disengaged my hand from hers and went and found a nurse. She made me a cup of tea and I used the loo. I drank the tea and went and stood by the lifts and smoked a bunch of cigarettes, one after another, and looked through the high windows over London. They went round three sides of the building. It was a panoramic view.

The sky was pearly lavender and the sun was setting over Battersea with a golden crash. A sliver of moon, the shape and colour of a fingernail cutting, was floating over Big Ben. The nurse came and found me and said that Wanda was getting worse. I went back into the room. She was awake again. Her eyes were bright and wet and her hands were claws that I held gently until she pulled them free and flapped them in front of her face and pulled at the bed covers and her nightgown to get at the wounds that hurt her so. Once or twice she looked at me with recognition and opened her gummy lips, and her tongue, white and swollen from the illness and the drugs that had been pumped into her, flicked over them. On those occasions I touched her mouth with a damp cloth which she sucked greedily but never spoke another word.

Outside in the corridor someone was whistling *The Star of the County Down*. It's the kind of tune you'd recognise right away, even if you didn't know its name and you were tone deaf. Whoever it was, was a real whistler and he'd chosen the right tune. As he went about his business he trilled and changed tempo, and as the afternoon and Wanda slowly died I sat next to her bed and held her hand and listened to that tune. I've never heard anything so beautiful or so mournful before or since. And as the tune and her spirit floated out over the river under that fingernail of moon, I realised she was right. The Kellermans deserved better than I'd given them.

I think she must have been dead for ten minutes before I knew she was gone. I could still feel the warmth in her skin but it was only the temperature of my hand radiated into hers. Finally I realised she was breathing no more, and called for the nurse with a voice that broke from bass to contralto. I saw the nurse through a veil of tears that I wiped away with the back of my hand, but no amount of wiping could stop them for long.

I felt a cold lump under my breastbone, and every time I think of Wanda now that cold lump comes back like a memory of pain I never felt properly.

I've cried for her since many times. But I know that my real time of crying is yet to come.

But at least I was there when she died. I was trying to give her some comfort. I was holding her hand when she finally couldn't take any more pain or suffering and her body closed down. Thank God I was. Some poor bastards aren't there when the ones they love die, and they have to live with that forever.

14

The staff came and took over and I was redundant. I got Wanda's belongings from one of the nurses. There wasn't much. A small suitcase containing a few clothes; a wash bag; her handbag containing her address book, her purse, her house keys and a note to me.

The nurse told me there would be a post mortem. I told her I knew.

I took Wanda's stuff to the pub over the road. God knows how many walking wounded the barman had seen in there, fresh from someone's deathbed or the morgue, looking to drown their sorrows. I would have bet I wasn't the first by a long way, and I sure wouldn't be the last. The boozer was half empty and I took my glass to a table and opened the letter.

Dear Nick,

If you read this, then I'm dead. And as I probably am, then you're reading it, if you know what I mean.

Poor Nick, I wonder if I can get through all this without telling you what's happening, or if I'll crack at the last minute and try to get in touch with you. That's in the lap of the gods and the hands of the surgeon. Same thing these days, I often think. And lately, Nick, I think too often, I think. Sorry, I'm rambling. Everyone tells me he's brilliant (the surgeon that is) but some things you can't cure by cutting lumps out.

If I don't see you, or can't, I want you to take care of everything. There's enough money for the funeral, you know where. I want to be cremated. No big deal. No flowers. All donations to the cats' home.

My cats are taken care of, or maybe you already know that. This is getting confusing.

Anyway, whatever. Goodbye and love,

Your friend,
Wanda

I was glad she'd wanted to see me, even if she had waited as long as possible to let me know.

That was the Wanda I remembered.

I sat and finished my drink and smoked a couple of cigarettes as it got darker, then I took her few things and left.

I stopped off at my place and let Cat in, fed him and let him out again. He'd be all right. I collected a change of clothes and a toothbrush and went to Wanda's house in Brixton.

It was fully dark by the time I got there. The house was terribly tidy and cold, even on that mild evening. I turned on the central heating. I'd never seen the place that neat when Wanda was alive. There were always cats all over the shop. The place still smelled of them, but you soon got used to it.

I walked through all the rooms turning on the lights as I went. It reminded me of the house in Crown Point. Lately I seemed to be doing a lot of walking through cold, lonely houses. Dead people's houses. I wasn't getting used to it.

The fridge was empty, turned off, and the door propped open. I shut the door, turned it on and went out to get some milk. The corner shop was still open. Thank God the people didn't recognise me as a friend of Wanda's. I didn't want to start explaining things just then.

I went back and made some tea and re-read her letter. I went to 'you know where', a loose brick in the old scullery. If I'd told her once, I'd told her a hundred times that it was a stupid place to leave cash but she'd never listened. It didn't matter much now. Under the brick was a thousand pounds in fifties and her will in a plain envelope. There was a covering note telling whomever it concerned that the original was lodged at her solicitor's, and their address. Every base covered. She'd left everything to me. The lot. The house and its contents, her personal jewellery that was in the bank for safe keeping, and an unspecified amount of money. Her solicitor was the executor.

I put the grand in my jacket pocket. She'd get a good send off with that. Then I realised that I didn't know any of her other friends. In fact, thinking about it, I didn't know much about her at all. She never talked much about her past. I used to pry, but she'd get the hump and in the end I left it alone. I got her address book out of her bag. It was jammed packed with names and numbers of all sorts – hotels, shops, newspapers – with names scribbled next to them that could have meant anything. There were lots of individual names too, with what I assumed were home phone numbers, but whether they were business or personal I had no way of knowing. Only one name meant anything to me apart from my own: John Rice, her ex-husband. That much I did know.

There were two numbers listed for him, one marked 'office', one marked 'home'. Both were 071 numbers. Central London, or at least what Telecom arbitrarily considered central London to be. I dialled his home number and a woman answered. 'Is John Rice there?' I asked.

'Yes. Can I tell him who's calling?'

'If it means anything, my name's Nick Sharman.' Obviously it didn't to her. 'I'll get him for you, Mr Sharman,' she said. She was gone for less than a minute when the phone was picked up again.

'John Rice speaking,' an anonymous male voice said.

'My name is Nick Sharman,' I said. 'I was a friend of your ex-wife's, Wanda.'

'So?' His voice was cool and it annoyed me.

'So, I *was* a friend because she's dead.'

'What?'

'You heard,' I said. 'She's dead. She died a few hours ago. I thought you might be interested.'

He ignored the last sentence. 'How?' he asked.

'An operation that went wrong.'

'Christ, I had no idea.' And I felt like a shit for giving him a hard time. If she hadn't told me, why should she have told anyone else?

'Nor did I,' I said.

'Christ,' he said again. 'Are you... ?'

I knew what he was getting at. 'No,' I said. 'A friend.'

'What's your name again?'

'Nick Sharman.'

'She mentioned you. She liked you.'

'I liked her.'

'A lot of people did. Years ago that was our trouble. I never believed she wasn't interested. I made a lot of mistakes.'

'Me too,' I said. 'One was not seeing her for months and not knowing she was ill. She's been ill a long time apparently. She kept it a secret.'

'She didn't tell me either,' said Rice. 'We spoke on the telephone sometimes. She called me at the office. My wife didn't understand.'

I bet you say that to all the girls, I thought.

'Look, I'd like to see you,' I said. 'I promised to arrange the funeral but I don't know who to ask. Her address book is thicker than the Gutenberg Bible.'

'That was Wanda,' said Rice. 'Everybody's friend.'

'But nobody's sweetheart.'

'Yes,' he said. 'Yes. Let's meet. When?'

'Tomorrow lunchtime?'

'Fine. Come to my office.' He gave me an address in Wardour Street and I jotted it next to his work number in Wanda's book. I wasn't going to throw it away.

I slept in her bed that night. It wasn't the first time, but the only other time I hadn't known anything about it. The sheets smelled of Wanda. I liked that.

I was up early and back home to change, and feed Cat again. Then I went to the undertakers. It was one of the most miserable experiences of my life. The boss was OK, a young bloke in a black suit, white shirt, black tie and black shoes. I explained what had happened. He told me the death certificate would probably take two or three days to come through, what with the PM and all. I told him I wanted him to take care of everything. All I had to do was choose the coffin. He showed me a book full of coloured photographs of them. I picked the most expensive of the bunch. It was the least I could do. I gave him my Access card and he filled out a slip and I signed it. I told him what Wanda wanted. He told me he'd handle everything, and that I should phone back later. I thanked him and left.

I got to John Rice's glass and chrome office where he was something in PR at ten to one, and he took me to a pub in Golden Square where we fought an engagement for a corner table and won. He went through her book indicating people he thought should be invited to the funeral. We had a couple of drinks and, although I thought he was a nice guy and I liked him, he was slightly awkward with me. I guessed we'd meet again at the funeral and that would be that. I left him and went back to Wanda's and phoned the undertaker. He told me everything was copacetic and the funeral would be in one week at Streatham cemetery. I thought about the Kellermans again.

I stayed on the phone and went through Wanda's book from A-Z. It was not the most pleasant of jobs. When I heard myself repeating the story for the twentieth time, and in a strange way beginning to almost relish it, I had a stiff drink.

By the evening I'd reached the majority of people and told them the time and place of the funeral.

15

After all that, I phoned Fiona. I hadn't seen or spoken to her since she'd walked out on me the night she'd found the photographs, although I'd thought about her constantly. Especially when Wanda had died.

'Hi,' I said when she answered.

'Hi yourself.' She sounded like she hadn't missed me. I'd missed her. Her tone made me feel even more miserable, if that was possible. I knew it was time either to start again or finish the whole thing.

'Wanda's dead,' I said.

'Who?'

'Wanda. The woman who looked after my cats.'

'Oh, Nick, I am sorry. What happened?'

'She'd been sick, very sick. I didn't know. She had an operation. It killed her.'

'I'm truly sorry,' she said. Her voice had changed. It was warmer and softer and more like the Fiona I knew.

'Me too. And I quit the case I was on.'

'Really?'

'Really.'

'Good. Those pictures were horrible. They scared me.'

'They scared me too,' I said. 'That's one of the reasons why I quit.'

'And the others?'

'Because you walked out on me.'

'Good,' she said. And I was glad she said it.

'What are you doing?'

'Nothing,' she said.

'Want to do something?'

'What?'

'A drink?'

'Sure, why not?'

'Now?'

'Sounds good.'

'I'll be round in half an hour,' I said.

'I'll be waiting.'

And she was. I drove to the block of flats in The Oval where she lived, and took the lift to the twenty-seventh floor, and she let me in through the security locks and chains. She looked beautiful. She was wearing a pair of ancient Levis, patched on one knee and worn to a hole on the other. Through the hole I could see she was wearing black tights underneath. With the jeans she wore a pink Levis shirt and black elastic-sided boots with Cuban heels.

'Looking good,' I said.

'Feeling good,' she said back. 'But you look like you've been through the wars.'

'Organising funerals for friends takes it out of you.'

'When did it happen?'

I told her.

'When's the funeral?'

I told her that too.

She held me tightly and it felt like coming home. 'You should have called before.'

'I didn't think we were on speaking terms.'

She kissed me with more passion than she had done for a long time. 'Don't be daft.'

'It's good to see you.'

'And you. Do you want to go out?'

'Not particularly. You?'

'No. There's booze here and most of a Deep Pan pizza from last night. Extra everything.'

'Sounds like you've really been living. Got any drugs?'

'I've got a bit of black.'

'How's the hot water?'

'Boiling, and lots of it.'

'Can I have a bath?'

'Sure.'

'Come and talk to me?'

'Of course. You run a bath. I'll roll a joint and make some Margaritas, then I'll be in.'

'Roll two joints and make a jug.'

'That kind of day?'

'That kind of life.'

She smiled. 'I'll even soap your back.'

'Deal,' I said.

I went upstairs to the bathroom. It was warm and smelled of Fiona. It was a fair size with a big tub, toilet and washbasin. I found a clean bath sheet in the airing cupboard and put it on the rail to warm up. I splashed a liberal squirt of Badedas bubble bath into the tub and put both taps on full. The hot water in Fiona's block was amazing. It was scalding hot at all hours and never ran out. It was the one good thing about the place apart from the view. The bubbles foamed up as I took off my clothes and hung them on the back of the door. I felt the water. Just right. I turned off the cold tap and stepped into the bath. I let the hot tap run on until the water was nearly up to the overflow and I could hardly bear the heat of the water. I turned off the tap and sank back under the pale yellow water. It was heaven. I could feel the stress kinks coming out of my muscles.

Fiona came in a couple of minutes later. The room was steamy and cosy. She was carrying a tray with a jug of Margaritas, two long-stemmed cocktail glasses rimed with salt, a couple of rolled joints, an ashtray and a box of matches. She put the tray on the floor, sat on the closed toilet seat, took off her boots and wriggled her toes and poured out two drinks the same colour as the bathwater. I'd have to remember not to get them mixed up. She passed me over one of the glasses. The liquid was ice cold and sharp with lemon and I felt more sweat bubble on my forehead.

'Pass me a towel, will you?' I said.

She did. I balanced my glass on the edge of the bath and dried my face and hands with the thick warm towelling. 'Light up, babe,' I said.

She put one of the joints between her lips and struck a match and set fire to the end. She inhaled and held the smoke in for five heartbeats, then let it out through her nostrils in two twin streams. 'Shit,' she said in a cracked voice, and passed the joint over. 'Strong little mother-fucker.'

'So's the booze,' I said, and dragged deeply at the joint. It was too. It cut into my throat and lungs. I felt the first hit like a club and sank lower into the water so that it lapped under my chin. 'Great,' I said. I came up and took another drag, passed the joint back to Fiona and picked up my drink. 'It's good to be here,' I said.

'It's good to see you.'

I sat in the bath for over an hour, topping it up with hot water every few minutes. We talked about everything except Wanda. As we talked Fiona plaited her hair into a thick rope of a pigtail and pinned it up on the top of her head.

By the time we'd finished both joints and the jug I was solid gone. I looked at her across the steamy room. 'Want to come in?'

'I thought you'd never ask,' she said, stood up and pulled the snap buttons on her shirt open with both hands. Underneath she was wearing a tiny white push-up bra. She reached behind her and undid the fastener and shrugged out of it. Her breasts looked as firm as tennis balls and I saw her nipples harden and grow. She undid the buttons on her jeans and pushed them and her tights and white panties over her hips in one motion and stood naked in front of me. Her skin was white and smooth and her triangle of pubic hair was thick and black and oily-looking between her legs. 'I suppose I get the tap end,' she said.

'Looks like it.'

'I'm going to get dimples in my back.'

'That'll be nice.'

She looked at herself in the full-length mirror behind the door. 'D'you think I'm getting fat?'

Dangerous question from any woman. From a model doubly dangerous. Fiona had never been skinny but there was something about her flesh that was different from most people's. It was soft but firm, like there was a layer of rubber between the skin and the meat below. But whatever I said I knew I was walking through a potential minefield, especially when I was so far out of my tree I was finding it difficult to enunciate the simplest of words. 'No,' I said.

'You sure?' She got hold of one buttock and squeezed a handful. 'Is that cellulite?' she said.

Really dangerous ground now. 'No,' I said.

'Liar!'

See what I mean? 'You're not getting fat, Fiona, but you're getting me at it, posing around like that.' She was too and she liked me telling her.

She walked over to the bath, folded up a towel and put it over the taps. 'You're no gentleman,' she said.

'And getting less so by the minute.'

She wrinkled her nose and stepped into the bath and sat down opposite me and pushed her legs alongside mine. I held her thighs in my hands. She felt so good. Her breasts floated on the water and I reached up and touched one. 'You're beautiful,' I said.

She put one hand between my legs. 'And I think you've been playing with a submarine in here. I've just found the periscope.' She knelt up, making a wave in the bath water that splashed over the side of the bath, and kissed me. Then she lifted up my cock and sat down on it. We both gasped as she slid down me. 'Hot,' she said.

I nodded and she moved up and down on me gently, trying not to spill too much water, until she came with a cry of delight. Her face and breasts were bright red and sweat had plastered her fringe on to her forehead. She pulled away from me and sat back down in the water. 'Nice,' she said. 'You can go now.'

I lay back and wished we had another jug of Margaritas.

Later on in bed together she let *me* get on top and then we ate cold, greasy pizza and shared a bottle of Bud. Then we did it again. It had been a long time. When we'd finished we lay back and shared a cigarette.

'Do you want tea?' she asked

'Love it.'

'I'll put the kettle on,' she said. That wasn't like her. She jumped out of bed and put on her dressing gown and went downstairs. I pulled on a clean T-shirt and boxer shorts that I'd brought with me. I sat up in bed and turned the sound on the TV up. I'd forgotten that *The Italian Job* was the late film. It was just starting. It's one of my favourites of all time. I must have seen it twenty or thirty times and I know great chunks of the dialogue off by heart.

Matt Monro was singing his heart out and Rossano Brazzi and his Ferrari were just about to get totalled on the front of a bulldozer in a tunnel in the Alps as I adjusted the volume. 'Put on your shades, Rossano,' I said to the screen. He did.

Into the tunnel he drove, turned a bend and – blammo!

'Tough shit, babe,' I said. 'One day you'll learn, and take the plane.'

'You and that bloody film,' said Fiona as she came in with two china mugs of tea and a packet of digestives on a tray. 'Don't you ever get tired of it?'

'Some films you don't.'

'I want to talk.'

'Can I just turn the sound down?'

'Sharman!'

Oh Christ, here we go, I thought. Now's the time to pay for your pleasure. I turned the sound off reluctantly as Noël Coward made his first appearance, and gave Fiona my full attention. 'What?' I said, dunking my digestive.

'I'm leaving the flat.'

'What, here?'

'Where else?'

'Why? I thought you liked it.'

'I do. I did. But I can afford a place of my own now.'

'Where?'

'I thought about Guildford.'

'Guildford?' I said. 'Why?'

'Why not?'

'Only one good thing comes out of Guildford,' I said.

'I know. The A3 to London,' she said back. 'Very funny.'

'All right, Guildford,' I said. 'Why not? There's some very nice properties around there.' Nice properties! I was still half stoned.

'There are. I've looked.'

'You never told me.'

'I'm telling you now.'

'Sure you are.' I was convinced this particular little scorpion was going to have a sting in its tail and I was right.

'What are you doing for money?' she asked.

'Living on my laurels.'

'I'll give you a week. Maximum.'

'Very amusing,' I said.

'What you do for a living is crap.'

'It's what I do,' I said. 'You said that to me once. Remember?'
She didn't want to. 'I've got a proposition for you,' she said.

'What – another fuck? I don't think I'm up to it.'

'Shut up, Sharman, and listen, will you?' I looked over her shoulder. Michael Caine was in a hotel room with about fifteen women. They were all in their underwear. It was one of my favourite parts of the film. Fiona saw me looking, hit the remote, and Michael and the ladies of the night vanished into the ether.

'You were saying,' I said, and lit a Silk Cut.

'Come and work with me.'

'What?'

'You may not have noticed but things are getting good for me. Very good. I've been offered a recording deal.'

'When?'

'Last week. Stock, Aitken and Waterman.'

'That's amazing.'

'And more modelling work than I can handle. And some acting. Maybe a movie. I'm going to be away a lot soon and I need someone with me. You could do it.'

'Do what?'

'Everything. Be my personal manager.'

'Like ironing your lingerie?'

'You like my lingerie.'

And I'd ironed it before when I'd found it in the washing basket at home with my stuff. I'm noted for my deft hand with silk. 'Ten percent?' I said.

'Whatever. Are you interested?'

'I don't know.'

'Look, Sharman, let's tell the truth for a change. You're wandering around like someone in a fog. You've got nothing.'

'I've got the flat and the car.'

'You chose that flat because it was the smallest in the world. You've done nothing with it. It came complete with everything. You didn't even choose the curtains. And your car's falling to pieces. You're not getting any younger, you know. Don't you think you're a bit old for all this nonsense? You'll end up dead in a gutter if you're not careful, and I'm fucked if I'm going to be the one to identify you at the morgue.'

That was a bit close to the bone, what with Wanda and all, but I got her drift. 'And Guildford?' I said.

'We could move in there together. I'm not going to get a two up, two down. I want a bit of room to breathe.'

And keep horses, I thought. 'It sounds idyllic.'

She looked for sarcasm in my tone. Couldn't find any, and didn't reply. I meant it. It did. For someone else. 'Can I think about it?' I asked.

'Of course. It'd be a hell of a change for both of us. But I need someone I can trust working for me.' It was 'for' now, not 'with'. 'Someone who won't fiddle the expenses and can keep his hands to himself.'

'I can't promise that.'

'You know what I mean.'

I did, unfortunately.

She yawned, 'I'm tired,' she said, and came into bed next to me, kissed me, and was asleep almost immediately. I've always envied people who can do that. I got up and opened the curtains and smoked a last cigarette looking at the lights of London far below me.

It had been a good evening. One of the last we'd ever have. There was more wrong than even I had realised. The sex had been good, but somehow it hadn't felt like a spontaneous display of love or affection, or even an attempt to comfort me at the death of a friend. It had been more like a tasty morsel you'd throw to a dog to make him behave, and could just as easily withhold if he didn't. I got the feeling that, if I agreed to jack in what I did, it would be the thin end of the wedge and that Fiona would take it as evidence that I could be easily manipulated in future.

Besides, I knew that I wasn't cut out for a career in showbiz. I got back into bed and put the TV back on and watched the end of the film. I've always maintained there was room there for a sequel.

16

There'd been better times and there'd been worse times in my life, but there'd rarely been lonelier times. The hours went by like they were frozen. I stayed indoors as much as possible. It was the thought of the price of shotgun cartridges that did it. I watched a lot of old movies on TV that week. BBC2 were running a Jack Lemmon season. I saw *The Apartment* and *Days of Wine and Roses*. Great films, but they just made me feel lonelier somehow.

I drank too much and went and scored an ounce of grass from under the railway bridge at Balham. It was a good deal. Lots of leaf and not too much stem or seeds.

I sat in front of the open window and let the soft early summer breeze blow away the smell of the dope whilst I looked out for strange cars parked up in the road outside.

I thought a lot too. About what Robber had said about staying on the case. But I made no firm decisions. As far as I was concerned it was finished. It was other people I was worried about.

The Sunday before the funeral I was sitting in the flat drinking a cup of coffee and reading the paper. Feeling weird and jittery as usual. The telephone rang. It was my ex-wife, Laura.

'Nick,' she said. I recognised her voice. Some things you never forget. That was exactly how she'd started the telephone conversation when she'd told me our marriage was finished.

'Laura,' I said back. That was exactly how I'd started the same conversation.

'Nick,' she said again, 'I wonder if you could do something for me?'

As far as I was concerned I'd already done all I could for her, bar opening my wrists. Perhaps that was the favour now. 'What?' I asked.

'Take Judith for a couple of weeks. Louis and I want to go away.'

Judith is my ten-year-old daughter. Louis is Laura's new husband. He's a dentist. Together they have a baby son.

'Where?' I asked. It was none of my business but she was trying to get round me so she didn't mention it. Normally she would have. 'There's a dentists' convention in Switzerland. Geneva. We're going to drive there. And on the way back we want to stop for a few days in France. At one of Louis's relatives.'

'A dentists' convention in Switzerland,' I said. 'The excitement could kill you.'

'Don't be sarcastic, Nick. You know I don't like it.'

'I know you don't like a lot of things,' I said. 'But you don't mind dumping our daughter on me when it suits you.'

'Is that how you feel about it? Dumping?'

'You know I don't. I don't get to see enough of Judith as it is. What are you doing with your son?' Once again it wasn't any of my business, but once again she didn't say so.

'He's staying with Louis's mother. She couldn't cope with Judith too. She's not as young as she was.'

Are any of us? I thought. 'Or doesn't want to,' I said.

Laura didn't say anything, which was answer enough. 'I don't know if this is a very good time,' I said.

'Typical!' she snapped. 'You're always moaning that you don't see her, and when you can it's not a very good time. When would be a good time then?'

'You don't understand…'

'Of course I don't. I never did understand you, did I, Nick?'

Christ, there's some things people *never* forget.

'Let's not go into that, Laura,' I said. 'We're not married now.'

'Thank Christ.'

It's strange to think that we used to love each other. That we used to look forward to being together. That we used to sleep in the same bed. I briefly wondered what she looked like naked these days, and couldn't imagine it. 'What about school?' I asked.

'One week is half term. I've got permission from the head mistress for her to be absent for the second week. They're setting her some homework, and I want you to make sure she does it. It's a good school,' she added defiantly.

It was. Better than anything I could have afforded, even at my peak. Which was a laugh. Private, with a uniform like something pre-war. But good. I couldn't take that away from it. 'And that suits you,' I said. 'Homework?' I knew I could never have kept Judith out of school for a week.

'She's very clever, Nick,' said Laura, ignoring the unspoken rebuke. 'Almost too clever.'

'That comes from my side of the family.'

'You can say that again! You always were too clever for your own good. I wish she wasn't. One day she'll trip and fall. She's not used to it. It'll hurt her more than if she was.'

'We'll have to see that she doesn't then.'

'No one can do that, Nick.' Which was true, but didn't stop you trying. 'So?' she asked.

'Of course she can stay.'

'You're *so* kind.' Now it was her that was being sarcastic, but I didn't mention it.

'So when are you going?' I asked. 'I have a few things to take care of.' I didn't tell her what.

'This Saturday. I'm sorry it's such short notice but the trip only came up yesterday.'

'That's fine,' I said. It was. It would take my mind off other things.

'Good. I'll get her and all her things over to your place after school on Friday.'

'Is she there now?' I asked.

'No, she's out with Louis. They go to car boot sales together at the weekend.'

'How suburban,' I said. Laura didn't take the bait, although I gave her every opportunity. 'Ask her to give me a ring, will you?'

'Of course. And thanks, Nick, I appreciate it.' Her tone was a lot softer now. Of course it was. She'd got her own way.

'It'll be my pleasure.'

'Bye, then. I'll talk to you soon.'

'Bye,' I said back, and waited for her to hang up first. It was something I always used to do.

She did. And when she had, so did I.

17

Wanda's funeral was very simple, just like she wanted. A small service and cremation. A lot of people turned up. The only one I knew was John Rice. Despite what she'd asked, a few people brought flowers. Me included. I laid a single white rose on her coffin. I didn't order a limo to follow the hearse. I didn't want to sit in it on my own. I followed it in my black E-Type Jaguar. I'd given it a good clean and waxing, and touched up the whitewalls. It must have looked a bit strange, but I think Wanda would have appreciated it.

It was a joyless occasion on a joyless day. It had rained overnight and early in the morning, but had stopped by noon. The clouds hung low over South London, and every tree and blade of grass at the cemetery seemed to drip moisture. After the service I stopped the car by the Kellermans' grave. The bunch of flowers I'd bought were still in the pot. They were long dead. The grave was beginning to look a bit unkempt as if there had been no visitors apart from me for weeks. I stood there for a minute, then went back to the car.

I'd arranged for a local pub where I knew the guv'nor to open its upstairs bar so that the mourners could drink her health.

About everyone who came to the service turned up for a drink. I didn't want to be the host, but as I'd arranged everything it seemed to fall to me by default.

Wanda had known a lot of people, and by my count most of them had taken time to come and see her off. She would have liked that. They seemed like a pretty mixed bunch. Some were in black, but a lot had dressed in bright colours which made the whole thing seem less like a funeral and more like a party.

The room I'd booked in the pub was chilly when I arrived. I felt a radiator and it was warm, but whether or not the heating was coming on or going off I had no way of telling.

The room was high-ceilinged and flock-wallpapered with a dashingly patterned carpet. Big windows were curtained with full-length maroon velvet curtains. I could see the cemetery through them. Along one wall was a highly polished wooden bar. Behind it were half a dozen spirit bottles on optic. On this side of the bar were a couple of tables with four chairs drawn up to each. There were more folding chairs stacked flat against the wall opposite. In one corner was a covered pool table, a rack of cues mounted on the wall next to it. The room had its own toilets. Two doors. A little sign on each. Silver, with a flat man or woman picked out in black.

Behind the bar were two real women, both in white blouses and black skirts. One was young with thick blonde hair and a vacant face whose jaw moved up and down, side to side, on a piece of gum. The other woman was older, thinner, tireder, with copper-coloured curls a few years too young for her and liver spots just starting on the backs of her hands. She wore a wedding ring. The younger one didn't.

I buttonholed Bob who ran the place, gave him my Access card and told him to give me a shout if the bill looked like going over five hundred quid. At that point it didn't seem likely. It was half pints or small measures of spirits all round. Voices were subdued and I asked the older woman behind the bar to put a tape on the sound system. She chose a Nat Cole album. It was perfect for the occasion. The tunes were old and sad, the strings lush, and his voice was that of heartbreak and lost dreams marinated in velvet liqueur. I asked her for a very large vodka and orange juice with lots of ice.

'Were you close?' she asked as she served me.

'Sorry?' I said.

'You know, to the deceased.'

'She wouldn't have liked you calling her that. But, yes, we were close. Just not as close as we could have been.'

'That's often the way until it's too late.'

'How true.'

'She must have been young?'

'About forty.'

'Such a shame.'

'You can say that again.'

'We get a lot of these. Being so near the cemetery,' she said. 'Funeral receptions, if that's what you call them.'

'I don't know,' I said. 'They used to call them wakes, didn't they?'

'A wake's before the funeral. Preferably with the body in an open coffin.'

'You know a lot.'

'I'm Irish,' she explained. 'We're famous for them. We seem to have more than our share of deaths.'

'I know the feeling.'

'Sorry,' she said. 'Of course you do.' She didn't know the half of it. 'There's sandwiches in the back,' she said, changing the subject. 'Will you let us know when you want them served?'

'A bit later, I think,' I said. 'When this lot have had a chance to get a few drinks down them. I'll give you a shout.'

'I'll be here.'

'I suppose I'd better go and talk to a few people.'

'Good luck.'

'Thanks.'

I took my glass and walked along the bar. The first person I came to was small, dark, female, in her midtwenties, with big round glasses, a black tailored suit with a very short skirt, high-heeled black patent leather shoes and dark tights on very good legs. 'Hello,' I said.

'Hello,' she said back, and smiled, showing even white teeth.

'I'm Sally.' She offered me her hand.

'I'm Nick Sharman,' I said. And took it.

She spoke in staccato sentences, very fast, like she had to be somewhere else half an hour ago. 'You're the one who phoned about the funeral. Thank you. I'd never have known about poor Wanda otherwise. I'm so glad to meet you. Although it could be under better circumstances. I hate funerals, don't you? I still can't believe it's true. I'm going to miss her so much. Were you her boyfriend?'

'No,' I replied. 'Just a friend.'

'There's no such thing as *just* a friend. Real friends are rare. What are your favourite daytime TV programmes?'

The change of direction in her conversation took me by surprise. '*The Magic Rabbits* and *Invitation to Love*,' I said without thinking.

'What a coincidence,' she said. 'Mine too.'

At the same time we both realised I was still holding her hand. 'You're supposed to give it back,' she said, and her eyes were big and green behind her glasses.

'Is that so? I must be out of practice.'

I let go of her hand. 'What are you drinking?' I asked.

'Irish. Straight, no chaser.'

'A real man's drink.'

She smiled and two dimples appeared, one in each cheek. 'That's right.'

'Do you want another?'

'Why not?'

I ordered her a re-fill from the blonde barmaid, got it and gave it to her. 'Thank you,' she said and raised her glass to me before taking a sip.

'Had you known Wanda long?' I asked.

'Years. We used to get together and drink gin and cry on each other's shoulders. I used to do most of the crying. I have problems with the opposite sex.'

Beating them off most likely, I thought, looking at her. 'Don't we all?' I said.

'I shouldn't have thought you'd have much trouble with women.'

'You'd be surprised.'

The look she gave me said that it took a lot to surprise *her*. I was prepared to believe it.

'What do you do, Nick? For a living, I mean.'

'At the moment, nothing.'

'Good job.'

'The hours aren't bad, but the money's lousy. You?'

'I'm in TV. PR at Thames.'

'Now that *does* sound like a good job.'

'It is. Big expenses. Long lunches. Fast cars.'

'You can take me to lunch sometime if you like.'

'Business or pleasure?'

'Whatever.'

'You've got my number,' she said. 'Use it. You can tell me all about your women troubles.'

'I will. But it would have to be a long lunch.'

She grinned and took a hit on the Irish. 'I've got all the time in the world.'

'Listen,' I said, 'I hate to drink and run, but I've got to go and talk to some of these people.'

'Are you deserting me?'

'Temporarily. I'll be back.'

'I'll hold you to that.'

'Count on it,' I said, smiled and went over to John Rice. I'd only had a chance to have a few words with him at the service. He'd looked pale and strained in the thin light from the chapel windows. If anything he looked worse now. He was talking to a stout party with a red face in a bad suit. Rice saw me coming and managed to raise the ghost of a smile.

'Nick,' he said. 'I'm glad to see you.'

'How are you, John?'

'Not too bad under the circumstances. I really didn't think I was going to take it so badly. You?'

'About the same. She was a tough one to lose.'

'You can say that again. I lost her years ago. I'm sorry I did. This is like losing her all over again.' His face tried to smile again, but this time it didn't happen. 'This is Dermot,' he said.

I shook hands with the big man. His grip was firm and dry. 'So sad,' he said. 'A real tragedy.' He was Irish. Southern, I guessed from the accent.

I agreed.

'I loved her, you know,' he said, and took a white handkerchief from the breast pocket of his jacket and blew his nose loudly.

'I don't know anyone who didn't,' I said. 'Did you know her for a long time?'

'Years. We met in Dublin. John here was over there on business with my company. We manufacture beer bottles, would you believe?'

With that belly and that complexion, I would.

'He brought her with him,' Dermot went on. 'She lit up that city like a torch. She lit up everywhere she went.'

I nodded. 'I've seen her do it.'

He shook his head and blew his nose again. 'When John told me she was dead, I flew straight over. I had to say my last farewells.'

I didn't know what to say. So I said nothing.

'It was a good turn out,' said Rice. 'At the chapel. Standing room only. Wanda would have got a kick out of that.'

'Yes,' I agreed. 'Is your... ?' It was an awkward question.

He looked at me and twigged. 'My wife? God, no. I think she only let me come so that she could be sure Wanda was dead.'

'That bad?' I asked.

'Worse, if anything. You've been married, haven't you?'

I nodded. I'd mentioned it when we'd met before.

'Then you probably know what I mean. Sometimes I wish I'd stayed single.'

I let it go. I didn't want to get on to the subject of my ex-wife. It might have curdled my orange juice.

'I'm going to wander round,' I said. 'Talk to some of these people. Thank them for coming. Not that I know any of them.'

'I do,' said Rice. 'Do you want any help? It would take my mind off things.'

'That would be great, John. If you don't mind.'

'And thanks for organising all this.'

'It wasn't through choice. You saw the letter she left.' We stood there awkwardly. Perhaps he was thinking the same as me: that Wanda hadn't asked him. 'I'll catch you later,' I said.

I walked round the room introducing myself to people I'd never met before, and probably wouldn't again. They all had their own stories about Wanda and I listened politely. I watched John Rice moving in the opposite direction. Every so often I broke off and went back to the bar for a re-fill.

There was certainly an interesting mix of people in the room. I hadn't invited all of them. John Rice must have gone through his address book and notified some. Others had heard the news from people I'd told and just turned up.

At one point I was talking to Wanda's dustman, the guy that had fitted her bathroom, and a geezer who wrote sit-coms for the BBC. They were engaged in a conversation about whether or not Elvis was really dead. The dustman was convinced he was alive and well living *à deux* with Jim Morrison in a turning off the Stockwell Road.

I also met Brian and David – no surnames please – who had run a design centre in Notting Hill in the sixties where Wanda had done some temporary work. They told me they were now doing very well in import/export in Docklands.

By about five the crowd had thinned a bit and those that were left looked like hard-core boozers. I called Bob over and ordered a drink. 'How are we going?' I asked.

'Your monkey went ages ago,' he said, almost rubbing his hands. 'But some other geezer – ' he stood on tip-toe and looked round the room ' – him,' he said, pointing to John Rice, 'stuck his American Express in for another, and his mate the Irish geezer gave me a couple of hundred cash. So we're all right. When that lot runs out, they can buy their own.'

'You're loving this, Bob, aren't you?'

'It's business, Nick. You've got to turn a coin. I'm sorry about your friend, I really am. Even though I never met the lady. I can see how it's cut you up. But life goes on. Listen, I'm sticking the sandwiches in for nixes and I'm doing the splits at cost, as it's you. I can't say fairer than that, can I?' He opened his arms and stood there with a quizzical look on his face and dared me to deny it.

I laughed. 'Sling in some pork pies and I'll believe you.'

'Done, son. And this drink's on your old mate Bob. Don't ever say I don't give you nothing. Drink your friend's health in heaven.' He got a triple vodka from the optic, added ice and orange juice and pushed it across the bar to me. I thanked him and took it and looked round the room. The place was buzzing nicely. Nat Cole was long gone and people were shouting to be heard above Madonna's greatest hits.

As I looked, the door to the room opened and a young woman's face, topped with very long, very blonde hair, looked through the gap. It was an unusual face. Not my idea of beautiful. But very attractive, and the hair was something else.

She pushed the door all the way open and came in. She looked about nineteen, but I guessed she was older. She was wearing a long black coat and black gloves which made her hair look even blonder by contrast. She stood in the doorway and I caught her eye, smiled and nodded. She came over. She had a big, jammy, sticky mouth smeared with bright red lipstick that clashed with her hair alarmingly. On some women it would have been a disaster. On her it was perfect. All of a sudden I wondered what it would be like to kiss that mouth. To be swallowed up and sucked in by it. 'Hello,' I said, when she got up close.

'Nasty twitch you've got there,' she said. 'Is it hereditary?'

Oh oh, I thought. One of those.

'No,' I replied.

'I'm looking for someone called Nick Sharman,' she said. Her voice was husky and deep and I was intrigued by the way her mouth moved when she spoke.

'You've found him.'

She put her hand on my arm. The pressure was only slight but I felt it all over. Her nails were painted bright scarlet. 'So you're Nick, are you?' she said. 'Wanda said you were a cutie pie.'

'Is that so?'

She moved a little closer and her fingers ran up the sleeve of my jacket like a posse of little red cockroaches. 'Sure is. I think she fancied you.' And she laughed throatily at the thought.

'Is that right?'

'But she said you were a little prim and proper.'

'Do what?' I said. 'Prim? Me?'

'That's what she said. And easy to tease.' She laughed out loud. 'I think she was right.'

I let her have her fun. 'Why are you looking for me?' I asked.

'Because you left a message on my machine. My name's Juanita O'Caine. I only got back from Paris this morning. I had no idea about Wanda. I didn't even know she was ill. I haven't seen her for ages.' She sounded guilty.

'Me neither,' I said to make her feel better. 'She didn't tell anyone.'

'When I got the message I came as soon as I could. I'm sorry I missed the service.'

'It wasn't all that…'

'Funerals rarely are.'

'What were you doing?' I changed the subject.

'What?'

'In Paris.'

'Business. I'm in publishing.'

'Books?'

'It *is* traditional. Since Caxton, I believe.'

'Are you always so sarcastic?' I asked. I didn't mind. I just wanted to know.

'No. I'm on my best behaviour today. Why? Does it bother you?'

She would have loved it if it did.

'Not in the least.'

'Good,' she said, and her lips pouted out with the word in a most attractive way. 'You must have taste.' She looked up from under long eyelashes and her eyes were the same colour as cornflowers. 'You've also got a lady friend, I believe?'

'Not so's you'd notice.'

'I'm sure you're being modest, Nick. Now is this party dry or is there any danger of me getting a drink sometime before the pub shuts?'

'What do you want?'

'Gin and tonic, please. A large one. Ice and lemon.'

I ordered up her drink. She looked round the room. I looked at her looking. When I'd been served I took it over to her. I asked her the name of the publisher she worked for. She told me. It was an old established firm with offices in Bloomsbury. We chatted for a few more minutes without saying much. Eventually she said, 'Do you know all these people?' taking in the crowd in the room with a glance.

'None of them really,' I replied. 'Well, I've said hello to a few. I met Wanda's ex last week. He's the longest acquaintance of mine in the room.'

'I've never met any of her friends either,' said Juanita. 'I think she was very good at compartmentalising her life.'

'Where *do* you know her from?' I asked.

'A restaurant. I was having a row with an ex of mine. He wasn't then. You know the kind of thing. All hissing and loud whispering.' I nodded. I knew the kind of thing only too well. 'She was with some bloke at the next table. We got talking. It was a relief after the row, I can tell you. We went to the ladies together and didn't go back. We ended up at some club being bought champagne by a sheikh.'

'Sounds good.'

'It was. Then he expected us to go back to his hotel. You know what I mean?'

'I can imagine.'

'So we played the same trick again. It became our party piece.'

'How long ago was that?'

'A couple of years. We'd see each other now and again.' She stopped. 'Well, we won't now, will we?' She stopped again. 'How did you meet her?'

'I was a cop. She was burgled. We went round.'

'We?'

'Another policeman and me. She got us pissed. I kept in touch. I always knew where to lodge a stray cat.'

'The cats,' she said. 'What happened to them?'

'They're fine,' I said, and came over weepy all of a sudden. It gets you like that, missing people when you least expect it. I excused myself and went to the gents. David and Brian, the entrepreneurs from Docklands, were in there. David was cutting out a line of rocky cocaine on the shelf above the hand basin. Import/export, I thought. Nothing changes. He looked up as I came in.

'Hello, Nick' he said. 'Come and have a blow.'

'Any good?' I asked.

'The best. Straight out of a Bolivian diplomatic bag.'

'You can't say any better than that.'

He passed me a rolled-up twenty. I leant forward and took a hit. I thought for a moment my eyeballs were going to pop out.

'Told you so,' he said.

When I went back out to the bar I had about eighty quid up my nose and felt no pain. I'd lost my drink so I went to the bar and ordered another. Suddenly I felt a tug at my sleeve. I looked round and saw Sally. She was carrying a tumbler two-thirds full of something that looked like neat Irish whiskey. 'You deserted me,' she said.

'I'm a cad,' I said back. 'What can I do to get back in your good books?' The dope and the booze I'd drunk had combined to put me in one of those moods.

'You're cheerful.'

'That's what funerals are for, aren't they?'

'Is that your girlfriend?'

'Who?'

'The blonde with the beautiful hair.'

'No. Just someone I bumped into, like ships colliding in the night.'

She laughed. 'You're stoned.'

I placed my hand on heart. 'You're right.'

'She's very attractive,' said Sally.

'She's got a wicked tongue.'

'So have I.' And she stuck hers into her glass lasciviously by way of illustration. I got her point. 'Do you think I should get contacts?' she changed the subject again.

'Why?'

'Men never make passes.'

'In your case, I doubt that.'

'Is that a pass?'

'If you like.'

'I like. But not tonight. I've got a date.'

'Who with?'

'Him over there. The tall one.'

I looked around and saw a good-looking fellow in a dark suit who was swaying to the music and spilling his drink all over the back of his hand.

'He's a psychiatrist,' she said.

'He's very drunk,' I said.

'I know. I'm going to take advantage of him.'

'Socially or professionally?' I asked. 'Physically or cerebrally?'

'Purely physically,' she replied. 'But you never know, I might get a free consultation out of it. Do you know how much shrinks charge these days?'

'I've always had mine on the National Health,' I said. 'Where are you going?'

'Freud's.'

'Are you serious?'

'Never more so. Look, I'm going to catch him before he falls over. Call me soon.'

'I will, Sally. I promise.'

She wiggled her fingers and pulled a sexy little face behind her bins and went off and snagged him. I watched them as they supported each other out of the room. The place was getting hot. I loosened my tie and followed them out. I turned left, away from the staircase and the direction they'd gone, and walked down the hallway to the fire exit that led out on to the flat roof of the saloon bar. The door was ajar. I pushed it open slowly. Juanita O'Caine was standing on the roof looking out over the lights of London that stretched away towards the river.

'Hello,' I said softly.

She spun round. 'Do you always creep up on people like that?' There was an edge of anger in her voice.

'I thought perhaps someone had found true love. I didn't want to disturb them.'

'Is there such a thing as true love?' she asked bitterly.

'Don't ask me. I'm no expert.'

'No? You looked to be doing all right with that bimbo in the specs in there.'

'Funny,' I said. 'She said almost the same thing about me and you.'

'Shows how much she knows,' she said dismissively.

'She's going out with a shrink,' I said.

'I thought she looked like she wanted her head examining, the way she was all over you.'

'He's taking her to the right place,' I said.

'Where? The insect house at London Zoo?'

'Bitch. Bitch. Bitch,' I said.

'What do you know?'

'Nothing. That's why I'm all alone tonight.' I leant on the parapet of the roof and lit a cigarette. 'Want one?' She nodded. I lit one for her. Just like in an old-time movie. Paul Henreid and Bette Davis. 'But my daughter is coming to visit soon.'

'Wanda told me you were a daddy.'

'Not a very good one, I'm afraid.'

'Better luck next time,' she said, and it hit home more than I liked.

'You're a piece of work,' I said. 'Do you know that? Some day someone's going to slap you so hard your teeth will rattle.'

'You?'

'No,' I said. 'I recognise the symptoms.'

'What symptoms?'

'Being so pissed off with yourself you've got to hurt someone else, just to feel a bit better.'

She looked at me closely in the faint light from the city. 'I'm sorry,' she said. 'That was a terrible thing to say about your daughter.'

'Forget it.'

'Will you get me another drink? I don't want to go back in there.'

A cool breeze was coming from the north and I could smell rain in the air. I was close enough to her almost to feel her shiver. 'You don't want to stay here either,' I said. 'There's another room inside. I expect it's open.'

I held her arm gently as I led her down another branch of the hall to a small room used for meetings of the local Rotary Club or something. I pushed open the door and switched on the lights. The room was furnished with one big table and half a dozen chairs. 'Wait here,' I said. 'Won't be long.'

I went back to the bar and ordered a gin and tonic and a vodka and orange juice. People were dancing now and someone had taken the top off the pool table and there was an energetic game of mixed doubles for drinks going on. The dustman was lying in a pool of spilt drinks and broken glass by the side of an upended table. He must have slid off his seat and taken it with him. No one was paying him a blind bit of attention. I checked his breathing and loosened his tie and left him. Perhaps he liked sleeping on wet carpets.

I collected the glasses from the barmaid and went out again. When I got back to the smaller room Juanita was sitting on one of the chairs staring into space. 'Reinforcements,' I said, and put the glasses down on the table.

She looked up at me with an expression on her face that would break your heart. 'You think I'm a cunt, don't you?'

'No,' I said.

'It's just that I have trouble expressing my emotions. Wanda understood.'

'She understood a lot.'

'You're right. I'm going to miss her.'

'Me too.'

'Got any more cigarettes?' she asked.

'Sure.' I gave her a Silk Cut and took one for myself. When I lit hers I saw smudgy tear tracks on her face in the light from the flame. She saw that I saw. 'Not a pretty sight,' she said.

'Suits me.'

'Don't give me your old bollocks, Nick. I've been propositioned by experts.'

For the second time that day I wanted to kiss her. I wanted to taste that jammy mouth and find out if it was as soft as it looked. I wanted to nibble on her lips, to lick her teeth and breathe her breath. I leant over and did it. She kissed me back. She tasted the way wet flowers smell. We kissed for a long time. When we stopped I felt dizzy and it wasn't just the coke and the booze. She took a drag on her cigarette and the smoke wreathed around her face and took on the colour of her hair. She looked like a fucking goddess.

I sat down opposite her and took a drink.

'Why did you stop?' she asked.

I shrugged.

'Principles, Nick? Wanda said you were very hot on principles.'

'Maybe,' I said. 'Or maybe I've just got too much luggage up here.' I tapped the side of my temple.

'It was nice,' she said. 'A nice moment in a lousy day. My trip to Paris was crap. Nothing went right. The flight home was a nightmare. I get a message to say one of my best friends, who I don't even know is ill, is dead. I miss the funeral. And now a man I want to kiss me won't.'

She started to cry, long deep painful sobs that ripped at her body. I went over and pulled a chair close to hers and sat and held her. It was awkward and uncomfortable to be honest. But it felt good. I kissed her again. She tasted of cigarette smoke. Cigarette smoke and wet flowers. It's an addictive mix. Try it sometime and see. I touched her hair. It was so fine I could hardly feel it. She bit down on my lip and I tasted blood. I ran my hands down her body. Her breasts were soft and hard at the same time. She was wearing a short black dress and dark tights. She kicked off her shoes. I ran my hand up the inside of her thighs. She parted her legs slightly. She felt hot and damp down there. I pushed the dress up to her waist and hooked my thumbs in the elastic of her tights and pulled them down. She lifted herself off her seat to help me. I pulled them down her legs and she kicked them free.

She was a natural blonde.

'What happened to your principles?' she asked.

'I think I checked them at the door.'

'With your luggage?'

'Probably.'

'Why don't you fuck me then?' she said. So I did. In that pokey little room on top of the polished table. It was great and all the more exciting for the thought that someone could come in and discover us at any moment.

When we'd finished I stood back and looked at her. She was lying on top of the table with one bare foot on the floor and one on the seat of a chair. 'That was nice, Nick,' she said, and slid one hand into her tangled pubic hair and wound a strand or two around her red finger nails. It nearly drove me crazy. I reached over and pulled her upright and kissed her again. She squirmed out of my arms. 'You're fucking my head up, Nick. I don't usually do this sort of thing.'

'Nor do I,' I said.

She bunched up her tights and pants and shoved them into her handbag and pushed her bare feet into her shoes. 'I think I'm going to go home.'

'Do you want me to come?'

'I don't think the bloke I live with would like that, do you?' She grinned. 'I think Wanda was wrong. I don't think you're prim and proper at all. Listen, give me a call. If I'm not there, leave a message. You know how to do that, don't you? If my boyfriend doesn't hear it first, I'll get right back to you.' She blew me a kiss and left. I sat down and lit another cigarette and finished my drink. It stung my lip where she'd bitten me. If it wasn't for that I might have thought I'd imagined the whole thing.

I went back to the bar and she and her coat were gone. I went and got another drink and bumped into the sitcom writer again.

We stood and discussed the rolling conspiracy theory on the murder of John Lennon and CIA activity in Central America during the late seventies and early eighties. The geezer was obsessed with dead pop stars. I listened to him droning on and thought about Juanita O'Caine.

I finally left about midnight. There was no possible way in this world I could drive. I abandoned my car in the car park and got a cab. Bob told me he'd keep an eye on it. I said I'd call back in the morning to pick up the car and my Access card.

18

I woke up with a lining of sandpaper between the delicate tissues of my brain and the inside of my skull. At least that's how it felt every time I moved my head. I was also carless and credit cardless and I had less than two quid in cash.

I got up and stood under the shower until I felt halfway human, dried myself off and shaved. Whoever it was in the mirror reminded me of someone I used to know. But not well. When I came out of the bathroom Cat was standing on the draining board in the kitchen looking like he was just about to commit hara-kiri in the garbage disposal unless he ate. As soon as he saw me, he started screeching. I fed him before I throttled him. I don't think I'll ever get used to the smell of tinned cat food in the morning.

Whilst he was gobbling down his Whiskas with Tuna I made tea and started to slowly co-ordinate. I thought about Juanita O'Caine as I dunked my teabag in my mug. Jesus, I didn't stop thinking about her. That was a very bad sign. She was just a kid. Half my age, give or take. I'd met her once, and we'd had a drunken fuck, and I was thinking about her. I hate that. Especially when it was obvious she didn't give a bag of beans for me. I hate that even more.

I didn't know if I felt guilty about cheating on Fiona. I wasn't even sure if I had. I didn't know if you could say we were still an item. Where do you draw the line? Perhaps I felt I was cheating on myself. Christ, but things had changed. When I was married I was the skirt chaser of the world. I felt cheated if I didn't have something going on the side. Nowadays I was more of a pussycat than a pussy hound.

I didn't want to think about it any more. I decided to go and get my car. I ordered a cab on a tab to drive me back to the pub. I gave the driver my two quid as a tip and promised to drop the fare in later. The cab office is next to mine. I've done it before.

During the ride, the cabbie wanted to talk. I didn't. I had other things to think about.

I thought about what Wanda had said about me giving up on the Kellerman case. I thought about how she hadn't given up on herself until she'd had no choice in the matter. And how bravely she'd fought it even then. It made me feel bad. I also thought about the Kellermans' grave in the cemetery being untended and the dead flowers in the pot. That made me feel even worse somehow. Maybe Wanda had been right. Maybe I was their last chance for peace. I shivered, and it wasn't just the hangover.

I thought about Fiona's offer for me to become her manager. It wasn't really me, let's face it. Although it was true that the job would have its advantages, I did best what I did best. At least that's what I told myself. Even if it did look like I'd lose her if I carried on doing it. I wondered what life would be like without her. Sadly, I came to the conclusion it would not be much different from the way it was now. Depressing thought.

I'd spoken to her several times and seen her once since she'd made the offer. She'd been great to me. Very sexy too. Just like her old self. But somehow it still came over like an act. I'd used the excuse of the funeral to delay giving her a decision on the job front. When I'd told her Judith was coming to stay, she'd got all excited. It made me kind of sad, as if I needed much to do that lately. Fiona had met Judith on a couple of my daughter's rare visits to see me, and they'd got on great.

When I got to the pub it was just opening. Bob was all smiles and bought me a drink. I wasn't surprised he had when he presented me with the bill and my Access card and slip. He said it was the best night he'd had for ages, what with us upstairs, and the darts team playing a home game in the public bar downstairs.

I bought him and the staff and myself a drink and signed the slip. He wanted to chat but I didn't, and was relieved when a driver and his mate came in with a delivery.

I took my beer to the table furthest away from the bar. I was the only customer at that early hour.

I sat there and let my beer get warm in front of me and thought about my life. And right then I made the decision that would change it, and the lives of many others. End some, and set others' free. I decided to go back on the Kellerman case.

19

I went back home and telephoned James Webb. He was as surprised to hear from me as I suppose I was that I'd called.

'I want to look a bit deeper into the case,' I said.

'Why? You couldn't wait to get off it as I remember.'

'I changed my mind.'

'Why?'

'I just did,' I said. 'Are you interested or not?'

'I've got the money if that's what you mean.'

'No money. I didn't give you value last time. This one's on me. Anyway, right now I'll only be doing it part-time.'

'Why's that?'

'Domestic responsibilities.'

'Well, if you're not charging…'

'I'm not.'

'Please yourself then.'

'Have you thought of anything else that might be relevant?'

'No.'

'Right,' I said. 'I'll go over the old ground first, and if anything turns up I'll let you know.'

'Fine,' he said.

'Fine,' I said back, and we both hung up.

Then I phoned Robber. He was in his office. The geezer always seemed to be working. I told him what I'd told Webb.

'Why?' he asked. Suddenly everyone was interested in my motives.

'Someone died,' I said.

'What?'

'Don't worry, it was natural causes,' I said. 'She was a friend. Before she died, she told me I gave up too quickly. She was right. So I've decided to have another go.'

'I hope you don't regret it.'

'So do I.'

'Take care, Sharman,' he said. He was changing his tune. It must have been my natural charm.

'I will.'

'And don't step on Detective Constable Hackett's toes if you see him. He doesn't like you.'

'I'm devastated,' I replied.

'Keep in touch.'

'Sure.'

And that was that. After he'd rung off I stood holding the phone, wondering where to start. Back at the beginning was probably best. So once again I pointed my car towards Crown Point.

I'd only seen half the neighbours and now was a good chance to get round to the rest. I went back to the house where the glamorous au pair lived, but this time there was no answer at all. Then I crossed over to the gates of an appealing little shack called Southfork. It was quite attractive if you fancied living inside a wedding cake. I walked up the drive and rang the bell. A woman came to the door. Her face said: 'We don't want any.' I smiled my most ingenuous smile and explained who I was. Her expression changed. 'Come in,' she said, and I did. 'Coffee?' she asked. 'I grind my own.'

I just bet you do, I thought. 'I never say no.'

'Go in there,' she said and indicated a large sitting room overlooking the back garden through patio doors. Everyone I was meeting lately seemed to have a patio except me. Maybe I hadn't got my life right.

Someone was moving about at the end of the garden, bending and straightening over a flower bed.

I sat on an uncomfortable sofa upholstered in a flower-patterned, thickly embroidered tapestry material and watched whoever it was slowly trundle a wheelbarrow from where he was working to a compost heap.

'Black or white?' asked my hostess who introduced herself as Babs when she returned. She was a fine-looking forty something with straight blonde hair cut short into a bob.

'White,' I replied as she put a tray on to a low table, knelt beside it, and poured the coffee. She had a nice backside in a tight grey skirt. There was no panty line as the material tightened across her buttocks, and I wondered if she was wearing anything underneath.

'Sugar?'

'One, please.'

She passed me a cup and saucer so fine that I could have broken it between my fingers like a sea shell. The coffee smelt good and I tasted it. It was good. 'Excellent,' I said.

'Nothing like it,' she said. 'I've got one of those flash machines that does everything but drink the stuff. My husband bought it for my birthday.'

'Nice thought.'

She pulled a face. 'He uses it more than I do.' She took her own coffee and sat on a matching couch opposite me. Her skirt was short and she showed me a good length of suntanned thigh *sans* stockings.

I didn't mind looking at her legs, but I didn't want to hear about how bad her marriage was, so I got straight down to business. 'Did you know the Kellermans well?' I asked.

'Yes,' she replied. 'Sandra used to pop in regularly. We were good friends. The children were wonderful. Such handsome boys.'

'It must have been quite a shock for you.'

'I was terrified for months afterwards,' she said. 'We almost moved. But we couldn't get a price for the house.'

My heart began to bleed.

'The people across the road did. I know how much they got. It was a scandal.'

All over the carpet.

'Did you see or hear anything that night?' I asked.

'No, I didn't. But I was here. The first thing I knew was when Geoffrey Godbold came running over and told me.'

'I spoke to him a few weeks back. His wife found the bodies,' I said.

Babs nodded.

'But no one saw or heard a thing?'

'Nothing. These houses are solidly built, and the gardens are extensive. You don't buy a place like this to listen to the neighbours.'

Not even when they're being brutally murdered, I thought. I finished my coffee.

She offered me another and I accepted. 'Of course, the police were all over the place for weeks,' she said.

I bet the coffee pot was working overtime then, I thought. She looked the type to love having a burly young copper or two around the place. It occurred to me that I should stop making value judgements. 'But you couldn't help them?'

'No.' She looked sad when she said it. I knew I was right.

'But maybe now, thinking back...' I was fishing and coming up empty.

'No, I'm sorry. And to think that whoever did it is still walking the streets. It makes me go quite cold.' She shivered as if to show me just how cold she could get. I wondered what would warm her up.

'And then the place was broken into,' I said.

'I know. It was awful.'

'Did you see or hear anything when that happened?'

'I'm always seeing and hearing things. My husband thinks I'm peculiar. We were going to get a dog. But the furniture…' She didn't finish the sentence and I made sympathetic noises.

'But nothing in particular?' I asked.

'We don't know exactly when it did get broken into. It was only when James came up to inspect the place that we found out.'

'You know James Webb?' I asked.

'Oh, yes. David and Sandra had lots of parties. James and his wife always came over.'

'What's his wife like?'

'Haven't you met her?'

'No,' I said. 'I'm just an employee.' I smiled shyly. I could tell she liked that because her skirt slid up another inch or two.

'Well, between us,' she said conspiratorially, 'she's a bit of a cow.' I imagined Babs would recognise one.

'Is that so?' I said. I wasn't really that interested but you never know when a bit of malicious gossip will help a case along.

'Yes. I don't think there was a lot of love lost between her and the rest of the family. But Jim, he's different.'

'How so?'

'Such a nice man. He doted on the family. Especially the boys. His wife couldn't, you know.'

I nodded.

'Well, couldn't or wouldn't,' she went on. I love bitches when they start to let their back hair down.

Just like you, Babs, I thought. The furniture, you know… 'Do you have any children?' I asked. She gave me a bit of an old-fashioned look. 'No, as a matter of fact I don't. You?'

'A daughter.'

'How old?'

'Elevenish.'

'You must be very proud.'

'I am,' I said. And that seemed to be an end to the conversation. 'Well, I must get on,' I said.

'Do you have to go?'

'I have other people to see.'

'Of course.' She looked disappointed.

'Thanks for the coffee,' I said, and put the cup on the table and stood up. She stood up too, and I saw more of her inner thigh as she did, and wished I could stay. But it was not to be. I shook her hand.

'If you need anything else, please call back,' she said. 'I'm always here in the afternoon. Me and the gardener.'

Lady Chatterley and the gamekeeper, I thought. 'Really?' I said.

She picked up my thought, and smiled and shook her head. 'You haven't seen him,' she said. 'Or smelt him.'

She showed me to the door. 'Thanks again,' I said. I walked down the drive and turned at the gate. She was still standing in the doorway. I waved. She waved back. I crossed the road. The name on the gatepost of the house opposite was Sierra Madre. No one was home.

I walked back from the front door to the street and saw an old boy standing at the gates of Southfork. He was grey-haired and stooped, wearing old trousers, Wellington boots, a tweed jacket with leather patches on the elbows and a squashy old hat.

'Are you the one asking about that house?' he asked and looked past me in the direction of the Kellermans'.

I nodded.

'She told me,' he said. 'Mrs Conway.'

'Babs.'

He nodded. 'I'm the gardener.'

He didn't smell so bad.

'You're a private detective?' he said.

I nodded again.

'Like on the telly?'

I shrugged.

'You've been in there?' he said and glanced over his shoulder.

'That's right.'

'She said. You want to watch her. You'll catch something if you're not careful.'

'I am careful,' I said.

'You'd be surprised the amount of young men call here.'

Young. That was complimentary. 'Would I?'

'Yes, you bloody would. Insurance men. Repair men. That's what she says. Bloody old tart! I see things.'

'I bet you do.'

'And know things.'

'I'm sure,' I said. I was getting tired of him by then.

'I know things about that house too.'

'What, the Kellermans'?' I said. A bit more interested, but not much. You get crap like that all the time when you're a copper. But I've learnt never to ignore it.

'Yes.'

'What kind of things?'

'All sorts.'

'You were here on the night of the murder?'

'No,' he said scornfully. 'I don't live here. I live in South Norwood. I was in the boozer.'

'So what do you know?'

'How much is it worth?'

I shook my head and made as if to pass him by. He grabbed my arm. His hand was hard through the material of my coat. 'I told you, I know things.'

'Like what?' I said. I was getting tired of his guessing games too.

'It's worth something.' He took his hand away. 'I'm not lying.'

I realised there was only one way to find out what he was talking about. I took some notes out of my pocket and peeled off two tens and gave them to him. 'Is that all?' he said.

'Tell me and we'll both know.'

'Some car's been here regular since the murder, sitting outside the gates. The driver just looks at the house. I see her when I'm doing the front.'

'Her?'

'Yes. A girl in a mini-car. Blue.'

'Dark blue?'

'That's right.'

'Do you know the number?' I asked.

He shook his head, suddenly disconsolate. The supergrass had blown it. 'There is something about it though,' he said.

'What?'

'There's a sticker in the window.'

'What kind of sticker?' I asked. Windsurfers do it standing up, probably, I thought. That cuts down the possibilities.

'An orange one.'

'In the front window?' I was suddenly interested.

'Yes,' he said.

'A round one with black writing?'

'That's right.'

Well, I'll be damned, I thought. A disabled sticker. And who was disabled and never called back? Why, the elusive Miss Hooper, that's who. Kellerman's secretary. I smiled and so did he, suddenly cheerful as he smelled more cash. 'How often is the car here?' I asked.

'Every few weeks.'

'Have you told anyone else?'

'No.'

'Not the police?'

'She didn't start coming till after the police had gone. I wouldn't tell them nothing anyway. I don't like the police.'

'Who does?' I asked.

He didn't reply.

'Thanks,' I said.

'So it was worth money?'

I nodded. More than I gave you, I thought. His face fell as I walked away. I stopped, took another tenner off the pile, turned and gave it to him 'Have a drink on me,' I said, and walked to my car.

20

By that time it was getting on and my hangover, which had receded slightly, was starting to bite again. I went back home and called Natalie Hooper, but the inevitable answerphone was on. It was obvious I'd have to go and see her in person. I looked up her address in my notebook. Epsom. I was in no mood to face the rush hour traffic out of town, and wanted to be fresh, so I decided to leave it until the morning. I made some cheese on toast and washed it down with a bottle of Rolling Rock and thought about David Kellerman's elusive and mysterious secretary.

I watched TV for a bit, but couldn't concentrate, and went to bed to rest my weary head.

I woke up early, feeling a great deal better than I had the previous day. I fed Cat and made myself a bacon sandwich for breakfast. I ate it watching a *Deputy Dawg* cartoon on TV. By ten-thirty I'd washed up and tidied the flat, and I decided to give Juanita O'Caine a call before I went out. Don't ask me why. Maybe I had a spiritual death wish. I looked up the number of the publisher she worked for in the book. I got through to the switchboard and asked for her extension. It rang three times before it was picked up.

'Hello,' said a woman's sharp voice. It was her. Even after such a brief relationship I would have recognised it anywhere. 'Juanita?' I said anyway. With a query at the end. Like you do.

'Yes?'

'It's Nick Sharman.'

'Who?' She knew.

'We met at Wanda's funeral.'

'Oh yes, I remember. Didn't we… ?'

'Yes.'

'Was it good for you?'

'Yes. You?'

'Adequate.' Fine. I set them up, she knocked them down. 'What do you want?' she asked.

She got straight to the point. I like that in a woman. To tell the truth, I didn't know what I wanted. I didn't say so. I like people to think I'm a positive kind of fellow. 'I thought we might get together.' It sounded pretty lame.

'Why ever would we want to do that?' she asked. It must have sounded pretty lame to her too.

'I don't know,' I said. 'Old time's sake, maybe.'

She laughed that throaty laugh of hers that sounded like she'd smoked too much, and drunk too much whisky, for fifty years, although she looked like she was barely out of her teens. It turned me on, even though I didn't really like her. Maybe that was why. Women I don't like often turn me on more than those I do. Always, come to think about it.

'There's always that,' she said.

'So?'

'All right, Nick. You can take me out to dinner. Somewhere very exclusive.'

'And expensive?'

'Naturally.'

'I'd better put my suit into the cleaners.'

'Good idea.'

'How's your boyfriend, by the way?'

'What boyfriend?'

'The one you live with.'

'I live alone. Always have. Probably always will. But I never invite anyone there until we've had at least one date. So I always tell strange men that I have a live-in lover.'

'Very wise,' I said.

'It saves giving offence.'

'And you wouldn't want to do that, would you?'

'Of course not.'

'So when's ours?' I asked.

'Our what?'

'First date.'

'Tonight?' she said.

'You move fast.'

'Not as fast as you, Nick, as I remember.' She laughed again. 'Will you pick me up?'

'Where do you live?' I said.

'Chelsea.'

'I should have guessed.'

'Why didn't you then?' She was as spikey as a hedgehog. That turned me on too.

'What's the address?' I asked.

She told me, and I wrote it next to her phone number in Wanda's book. 'I'll call round for you. Is there any particular place you'd like to go?'

She told me. At the mention of the restaurant's name my Access card gave a shudder. 'We can walk there from here,' she said.

That would be the only economy of the evening. 'I'll book a table,' I said. 'Eight o'clock?'

'Suits me.'

'Am I invited for cocktails before dinner?' I was getting daring. She considered it. I could hear her breathing down the phone and I wished that I could taste her breath again. 'Sure, why not? Seven suit you?'

'I'll be there,' I said. Try and keep me away, I thought. I really was a glutton for punishment.

'See you later then,' she said. 'Bye now.' And she hung up.

21

I put the receiver down, put on my jacket, went downstairs to the car and drove to Epsom. The road I wanted was on the outskirts of the town. I had to ask three people before someone knew its whereabouts. It was part of a new estate, a bungalow at the end of a row of similar single-storeyed houses. Next to a building site that looked like the crew had downed tools one lunchtime and never gone back. The development was all too raw and freshly landscaped for my taste, but what do I know?

One thing I did know was that I was at the right place. There was a dark blue Mini with a disabled sticker in the windscreen, parked in the short drive in front of the garage. A look inside showed the controls had been altered for someone who couldn't use their legs. Also, it was the only house in the road with a ramp running up to the front door instead of steps. I walked up it and rang the bell. It was at knee height. I stood there for a minute, then rang again. I heard a woman's voice from the other side of the front door.

'Who is it?' she called.

'Nick Sharman,' I replied.

'That means nothing to me.'

'You should check your machine,' I said. 'I called and left several messages a few weeks ago. And I called again last night.'

'What about?'

'David Kellerman.'

There was a long silence. 'Who are you?' she asked eventually.

'I'm a private detective from London. I'm working for James Webb, Kellerman's brother-in-law, looking into the circumstances of the murders. Listen, do I have to shout through the door? I don't want to discuss it like this. Why don't you let me in?' Silence again.

Then there was a rattle of chains, and the sound of locks turning, and the door opened. In front of me was a woman in a wheelchair. About twenty-five. Brown hair. A heart-shaped face that showed no emotion. Dead eyes. A body shrouded in a big cardigan so that you couldn't tell if she was fat or thin, and legs covered with a Black Watch Tartan blanket.

'What do you want?' she asked.

'To talk.'

'About Mr Kellerman? Why? Why now? It's been such a long time. What do you want to talk about? Has something happened?'

I only answered her last question. 'No, nothing's happened. That's why James Webb hired me.'

'So why are you *here*?' She emphasised the last word.

'Like I said, to talk to you.'

'What do you want to talk about?'

'About anything you know.'

'I know nothing,' she said.

'You worked for Kellerman.'

'So?'

'So maybe you can help me.'

'I doubt it.'

'Can I come in anyway?'

'How do I know?' she asked.

I didn't get her drift. 'What?'

'That you are who you say you are.'

'You don't,' I said, and took my wallet from my inside jacket pocket and one of my cards from inside it. I gave the card to her. She took it in one of her strong hands, with short, unvarnished nails and fingers devoid of rings, and as she read it she creased the card.

'This means nothing,' she said.

'What does?' I asked. 'But I am who it says I am. Telephone James Webb if you don't believe me. I just want to talk to you for a few minutes. I'm not here to hurt you, Miss Hooper. Just a few questions and I'll be gone.'

I thought she was going to refuse. Then she said, 'If you must,' and wheeled the chair out of my way. I stepped into the hall and closed the door behind me. 'The police questioned me several times when it all happened. Why dig it all up again?' she said.

'The police haven't solved the case. James Webb asked me to look into it again, independently.' I didn't tell her about Stan McKilkenney and the fact that the case was live again.

'What good does asking me the same questions all over again do?' she asked dully.

'They might not be the same questions,' I said.

'You'd better come through,' she said, and wheeled herself backwards down the hall and through a wide doorway into a sitting room. I followed. No patio doors here. Just a window looking over a patch of garden that was black dirt. She nodded at a dark blue velvet-covered armchair. I used it.

'Do you want a cup of tea?' she asked.

'Yes,' I said. 'I'll make it if you like.'

'Don't be ridiculous,' she said. 'I am capable, you know. Especially of making a cup of bloody tea.' For the first time her eyes showed some sign of life.

'One sugar,' I said.

She wheeled herself into the kitchen that opened straight off the sitting room with no connecting door. All the work surfaces were at wheelchair height. I noticed that all the switches and plug sockets in the sitting room were the same. The inside of the place had been custom built for a disabled person. Expensive. Especially for a secretary who had time to visit her late employer's house regularly on working days and was at home on a weekday afternoon.

'Where did the police question you?' I asked.

'At the office twice, and once at the police station.'

'Not here?'

'No.'

'But you were living here then?'

'I'd just moved in.'

'Nice place.'

'It does me.'

'Where were you living before?'

'At home with my mum and dad.'

'Why did you move?'

'They were too restrictive. They treated me like a kid. I wanted some freedom.'

'Are you working now?'

'No. I'm on the social.'

'You didn't bother getting another job?'

'Bother? Christ! Jobs aren't that easy to get, not for people like me. Not all employers are as understanding as David was.'

It was David now, I noticed. Not Mr Kellerman. I sat in the chair and watched her in the kitchen as she boiled the kettle, made the tea, and poured out two cups from the pot.

'Come and get your tea,' she said.

I did, and went back to the chair and put the cup and saucer on a table beside it. She fitted a small tray on to one of the arms of the wheelchair, and put her own cup and saucer on it. Then wheeled herself back into the sitting room and manoeuvred the chair until she was facing me from the other side of the dead fireplace.

'Have you got any cigarettes?' she asked. 'I haven't been out today.'

'Sure,' I said, and took a packet of Silk Cut and my lighter from my jacket pocket. She pushed herself forward and took one. I lit it for her. She wheeled back to the other side of the fireplace and sipped at her tea. I lit a cigarette for myself. 'Do you have an ashtray?' I asked.

'In the kitchen on the draining board. There's two. Bring me one, will you?' I went and got them. A matching pair from Harrods. I didn't know where to put hers. 'On my lap,' she said. I put one of the ashtrays on the blanket. It was an oddly intimate thing to do. I put the other ashtray on the arm of my chair and sat down again.

She smoked and looked at me. I smoked and looked at her, and the smoke was like a grey veil between us.

'How long did you work for Kellerman?' I asked.

'Three years.'

'Before that?'

'Secretarial college.'

'First job?'

'Only job.'

'You were his private secretary?'

'PA.'

'So you knew everything that went on?'

'I don't follow.'

'Somebody killed him, his wife and two children. I've seen the photos. It wasn't pleasant. Someone didn't like him, to put it mildly. You worked for him. You might know that someone.'

'I don't think I know anyone who could do a thing like that.'

'He owed money,' I said.

'Who doesn't? Business was bad at the end. Recession, you know. It hit the retail sector badly. He had a big overdraft. His business wasn't the only one. And I'm sure it's just as bad for small businesses now, if not worse.'

'I spoke to your old accountant. He wasn't very forthcoming. But he did tell me that he thought there was more money around than there should have been. And then suddenly, nothing.'

'I'm afraid I don't know anything about that.'

'I know there were bank loans,' I said. 'Were there any private ones? Loan sharks who wanted their money back and took it in kind with shotguns, when they found out that the business was going bust?'

'I told you, I don't know.'

'You should do, being his PA.'

'I didn't know everything about him.'

I changed tack. 'Did he have a girlfriend?' I asked. She went white and dropped her cigarette. It rolled across the carpet towards me. I leant over and picked it up, then gave it back to her. When our fingers touched I felt an electric shock, like static. I could tell she felt it too.

'What do you mean?' she asked.

'Was he screwing around?'

'No. He was a good man.'

'Give me a break. Did he have a woman on the side? A married woman maybe, and the husband turned out to be more than Kellerman could handle?'

'No.'

'You seem sure for someone who "didn't know everything about him",' I said.

'I keep telling you, I don't know. The police went through this with me several times.'

'What policeman?' I asked.

'I can't remember.'

'Robber?' I asked. 'Inspector Robber.'

'That was him,' she said. 'A nasty man. He gave me the creeps.'

'You and a million others.'

She stubbed out her cigarette and leant down and put the ashtray on the fireplace.

As I watched her I knew I was missing something. Something important. I looked around the room. In one corner, up close to the ceiling, a tiny spider was spinning a web. It swung on its silken thread back and forth. For a second or two I watched it building a trap for the unwary.

'He said you were stupid,' I said.

'Who?'

'The Inspector.'

'Did he?'

'Yes, he did. In fact, he called you a poor, twisted, stupid spastic as I recall. A raspberry ripple. Do you know what that means?'

'Yes, I do. How nice of him.'

She didn't change her expression, but she went whiter if that were possible, and I saw that her hands were trembling. She saw me looking, and clasped them together to keep them still. I felt like a bastard putting her through it. But I kept on: 'I expect you're used to that, though, looking the way you do.'

'What way's that?' Her voice was thick.

'Plain, dowdy and put upon. At least, that's the impression you gave Robber. Stupid. Twisted up. But you're not, are you?'

'Aren't I?'

'None of those things. Not poor either. Not by the looks of this place. Who paid for it?'

'That's none of your business. I think you should go now.'

'Is that right?' I said.

'Yes.'

'And if I don't?'

'I'll call the police.'

'Why don't you call Robber? Get him over here. I'm sure he'd love to renew his acquaintanceship with you after all this time. Ask you how come you've got a nice place like this, on what the government pays.'

She looked over at the telephone and then back to me. 'Why are you persecuting me?'

'I'm not. I just resent you treating me as if I'm as stupid as you'd like everyone to think you are. You're a bit out of practice, Miss Hooper. You're not doing the job very well today.'

'What?' Her eyes blazed and colour came back into her skin and she wasn't half bad-looking.

'You're not stupid at all, are you?'

'Not as stupid as your friend Robber. He only saw the chair, not who was in it.'

'Robber is no friend of mine, believe me. So did Kellerman pay for all this? Is this where the money went?'

'I paid for it.'

'With what? Your Giro?'

'I've got private means.'

'Prove it.'

'I don't have to. Not to you.'

'Maybe to the police. The case isn't closed. Never will be.'

She looked at me again. 'David is dead and that's an end to it,' she said.

'I smiled. 'No,' I said. 'Not an end at all.'

'What do you mean?'

I changed tack again. 'Do you visit the grave?' I asked.

'What grave?'

'The Kellerman family's.'

'No.'

'I bet you do. I have. Twice. It's a sad place.'

'Graves usually are.'

'Not always.'

'Why should I go there anyway?' I knew she'd have to ask.

'You visit his house,' I said.

She looked shocked. 'No,' she said.

'Yes, you do.'

'I don't.' But it was a weak denial.

'I saw you,' I said. 'I didn't know it was you at the time, but I saw you.'

'Rubbish!'

'It was your car. And I'm not the only one. The old boy who prunes the roses over the road has seen you too. Every couple of weeks since the police left, he says.'

She bowed her head and I could see her scalp, pale and clean-looking, in the parting in her brown hair. 'I told you, he was a good man.'

It suddenly clicked. It shouldn't have taken so long. I was out of practice. 'Were you lovers?' I asked.

She looked up and there were tears in her eyes. 'And if we were?' I didn't answer.

Her top lip curled scornfully. 'Or isn't that allowed in your world? Only people with perfect bodies can make love, is that it? Does it embarrass you, or turn you on a little bit?'

I didn't answer again. I sensed a tide of pent-up emotion behind the cardigan and the sensible hair and the lack of make up and jewellery. I'd felt it first when I put the ashtray on her lap and again when our hands had touched. I wanted that emotion out in the open.

That's what I miss most about being a copper. A real copper. A detective. Asking questions. Being nice, or being nasty. Sometimes both. Digging out things that other people can't see. Things that other people want to keep hidden. People a lot smarter than I'll ever be. I was good at it. Excellent. It's a gift. I had it. It's like another sense. I knew what made people tick. What they loved and what they feared. I knew what buttons to press and sometimes it scared the shit out of me.

I was a Detective Constable for a long time. And I passed my Sergeant's exams too. But my interim reports were always lousy.

It didn't worry me. I didn't want promotion. I wanted to sit in little rooms that stank of fear and fags and feet, and look deep into people's insides and dredge out emotions they sometimes didn't even know they had themselves. That's power, and I had it.

A DC is the best job on the force. No responsibilities – not many, anyway. Not much money either. That's the trouble. Not that you can't make it up. I did. I justified it by pretending it didn't matter. But it did. It lost me the power. When I think of those people who turned me bent. Those fuckers with the envelopes full of high-denomination currency. Those bastards with their 'Take the money and go away and play, little man' attitudes. Those shitheads who just love having a copper in their pockets. The ones who knew I had the power and took it away. When I think of them, I want to get all the money I took and go back and mash it down their throats until they choke. They took everything I valued and trod all over it in their handmade Italian shoes. And I let them.

The silence stretched and I looked at her. Always let them speak first, that's one of the rules. And they always do.

'Well, does it?' she asked.

I shrugged.

'He said I had a beautiful body. Can you believe that? He was the only man who's ever said that to me. Beautiful legs. Even though they're dead. Do you want to see?' She pushed the rug off her knees. Underneath she was wearing a long skirt buttoned up the front. She pulled it up. She was wearing short woollen socks but her legs were bare. Bare and blue-white and cold-looking. But he had been right, they were beautiful. She slapped one knee and it sounded like she'd slapped a piece of meat. 'Not bad, are they?' she said. 'Pity they don't work. Everything else does. Want to see?' She pulled the skirt higher.

I felt ashamed. 'Stop,' I said.

'Not got the nerve, have you? Are you frightened? Don't worry, it's not catching. It's all there. All the bits that ordinary women have. Next time you're fucking some girl think of it. I'm as warm and wet in there as any normal woman. Wetter probably. Want to try it? Or my mouth? David said I had the dirtiest mouth he'd ever known. Not like that cold bitch of a wife of his.'

I felt terribly sorry for her all of a sudden. That was the other side of the coin. The empathy I felt for other people sometimes blew those emotions I'd uncovered back on to me. I got out of my chair and knelt beside hers. I separated her hands, one from the other, and I held them in mine. They felt as cold as her legs looked. But there was that charge between us again, when we touched. Our faces were less than two feet apart. All of a sudden she started to cry. Noiselessly. The tears just rolled down her face and dripped off her chin.

'Don't,' I said.

'I loved him. I've never loved anyone else. He was going to leave her and come and live with me. He loved me too. He called me his baby. He didn't mind about me being what I am. He liked it. He could do things for me.'

'I know he did,' I said. 'I know. Don't cry, baby.'

She started to cry harder when I said that. I held her and stroked her hair. I seemed to be doing a lot of that lately.

She pulled away and sniffed. 'Will you get the tissues?' she said. 'Over there.' There was a box of Kleenex for Men next to the telephone. I got it for her and she took a handful and wiped her eyes and blew her nose.

'Better?' I said.

She smiled.

'So did he pay for all this?' I asked softly.

'What if he did? It was his money.'

'Not entirely. How long was it going on?'

'What?'

'You and him.'

'A couple of years.'

'Did anyone else know?'

'No. They all thought like your policeman. People don't see the disabled as having emotions. They're just there to be pitied.'

'But not David Kellerman?'

'No, not him. He saw the real me.'

'Where did you do it?' I asked.

'What do you mean?'

'You were moving in here when he was killed. Where did you meet before? Not where you were living with your mother and father, I'll bet.'

'At work.'

'Nowhere else?'

'No.'

'You're lying,' I said. 'You don't have to tell any more lies, Natalie. Trust me.'

'I'm not telling lies,' she said. But she couldn't lie to me any more.

'Yes, you are,' I said gently. 'I don't believe a man like him, or a woman like you for that matter, did it on the office sofa for two years.'

She gave in. I actually saw her sag in the chair. 'You're right. There *was* another place.'

'Where?'

'A cottage. Outside East Grinstead. It was ridiculous. I couldn't get the chair through the front door. He had to carry me in.'

'Was it rented?'

'No, it belonged to David.'

'So what happened to it when he died?'

'Nothing.'

'What? It's just standing empty?'

'Yes. He kept the ownership secret. He had to. We were going to live there together. But, like I said, it was a ridiculous place. He bought it as a surprise for me. He didn't think about the logistics of it at all. So he bought this place instead. He made sure it was right for me. Just one floor. Everything designed for someone in a wheelchair. He even put it in my name. It was as if he knew what was going to happen to him.'

I raised my head and sniffed the air. Perhaps he did, I thought. Perhaps he did.

'I thought he'd sell the cottage right away.' She went on. 'But he kept it. He said it was our hedge against inflation. I never really understood what he meant by that. The property market collapsed, you see, soon after. I suppose he was going to sell it when the market improved again.'

'And it's still there, empty?'

'I've already said that.'

'Did he make any other provisions for you when he bought this place?' I asked.

She looked away and blushed.

'Did he?' I asked again. 'It might be important.'

'Yes. He put some money in a high-interest account. No one knows. The Social Security...' She didn't finish the sentence.

'That's what you live on?' I said.

'The interest, yes. I won't have to give it back, will I?'

'I won't tell them, if that's what you mean,' I said. 'I'm no great fan of the Soche myself.'

'Thank you,' she said.

'Do you happen to know where the deeds to the cottage are?' I asked.

'He kept them there, I'm sure. Why?'

'Because James Webb inherited Kellerman's estate. And he ended up with not a lot. He never mentioned a cottage, or anything like that. If he knew about it, I'm sure it would be on the market. Perhaps if I can find the deeds and give them to Webb, I won't have to tell him about the money Kellerman gave you.'

'They must still be there. The place isn't for sale, I'm quite certain of that.'

'You've been there recently?'

'Not inside. I've driven down there. Like I go to his other house in Crown Point. It seems to bring him closer somehow, even though those horrible things happened there. But I told you, I couldn't get into the cottage if I wanted to.'

'Have you got a key?' I asked.

'Yes. Why?'

'I'd like to see the place.'

'Why?'

'Curiosity.'

She thought about it. 'Will you take me?' she asked.

'Yes,' I said. 'But let me go on my own first.'

'Why?'

I shrugged. 'I want to see it just as you left it. No distractions.'

'Would I be a distraction?' she asked, and there was flirtation in her voice and eyes.

'Probably.'

'But you will take me? Promise.'

'Of course.'

'All right.' She rolled herself over to a bureau against the wall, next to the window, pulled open a drawer and took out a Yale key on a key ring. She came over to me. I took the key from her. Our fingers touched again and I got another tiny charge of static and she looked into my eyes. We were very close in that small room and I felt a sudden surge of desire for her. She knew, and smiled and wheeled herself away. She'd won that small battle. I put the key in my pocket.

'You'll need the address,' she said. I took out my notebook and wrote it down as she told me, plus instructions on how to get there from East Grinstead itself. I put my notebook back in my pocket. 'I'll be going now,' I said.

'You will come back and see me again?'

'I said so, didn't I?'

'I'll wear something special for you if you do, and show you what I can do with my mouth.'

'I'll remember that,' I said. And knew that I would. 'I'll see myself out.' I leant down and kissed her on the cheek. 'Goodbye, Natalie.'

'Goodbye.'

I left her my cigarettes on the tray attached to the arm of her wheelchair.

I could feel her eyes on my back as I went.

I sat outside in the car for a few minutes. I was getting a headache. That often happened when I'd been questioning people. I sat and thought about Natalie Hooper. I wondered if she'd told me everything she knew. She hadn't been lying to me, of that I was certain. Not that people couldn't lie to me – I'd been lied to by the best of them – but she wanted to talk, needed to talk to someone. Only Robber never had a chance with her. He was all wrong for the job. I just wondered if she'd retained some little secret close to her heart to keep her warm at night.

I took the key to the cottage out of my pocket and looked at it, then my watch. Time had flown. I didn't feel like driving to East Grinstead and finding some lonely cottage and turning it over. My head hurt, I had a heavy date and hadn't booked the table yet. And Judith was arriving the next day and I still had things to do.

I decided I'd go after the weekend. What was the rush after all? I had all the time in the world.

And on such slight considerations, whole nations have been lost.

22

When I got back to the flat, the telephone was ringing. I picked it up. It was James Webb.

'Hello, Jim,' I said.

'How's it going?' he asked.

He sounded so miserable I decided to give him the good news.

'Not bad,' I said.

'Have you found something?'

'I might have. I talked to an old boy who does the gardening at one of the houses on the close. He put me on to something.'

'What?'

'Have patience, Jim. Bear with me. I'm going to check it out on Monday.'

'No sooner?'

'It may be nothing. I told you I've got some domestic responsibilities to sort out. It's only a couple of days. I'll talk to you Tuesday. OK?'

'It'll have to be, won't it?'

'Don't worry, Jim. I promise you'll be the first to know. Listen, I've got to go. I'll talk to you next week.'

'Fine,' he said, and hung up.

I lit a Silk Cut and picked up the phone to call the restaurant.

I arrived at the address Juanita O'Caine had given to me at 6.59 precisely. I parked on a single yellow line just opposite. It was a fine old Georgian terraced house split into three flats. Hers was in the basement.

I'd chosen what to wear carefully. A dark grey, almost black suit in a loose, hopsack weave, double breasted, with turn-ups on the pants. A white button-down, Oxford cloth shirt with double cuffs, black elastic-sided boots and a tie that was an explosion of bright primary colours. I looked pretty good.

I walked down the entry steps to her door and rang the bell. It only took her five minutes to answer. It did occur to me that she'd gone out and just forgotten all about me. Or just gone out.

When she finally got round to opening the door she looked amazing. She was wearing a black velvet evening dress. Short, tight, and cut so low that the bodice seemed to defy gravity as it hung off the tips of her breasts just above the aureoles of her nipples. Her blonde hair hung straight down her back. She had on what looked suspiciously like a real diamond necklace and matching earrings. If they *were* real I'd've swapped them for my flat there and then, and expected to make a profit on the deal.

'Hello,' she said with a smile that out-dazzled the ice she was wearing. 'I wasn't ready.'

'I nearly went home,' I said.

'No, you didn't,' she said. 'Come on in.'

She was cooler than ice too. But you know what they say: Life's a bitch and then you meet one.

She walked down the short hall of the flat, and I went in and closed the front door behind me and followed her. It was dark inside, and smelled of her perfume. She led me into the living room. It was a garden flat, the garden being a storey lower than the pavement outside. I looked round the room. It was minimally furnished. The floor was polished wood, and bare except for one rug that looked as expensive as it was ancient. There was a sofa and matching armchair upholstered in a dark red slubbed material. The TV was Bang & Olufson. So was the video and CD system. There were about a thousand compact discs on shelves on one wall. About a thousand books on shelves on another. The spotlights were pink and that was about it. Juanita obviously had money and taste. What the fuck did she invite me round for? Mind you, I could learn to live with it.

Fat chance, I thought.

She turned on one high heel and looked at me. I didn't know if she liked what she saw. I did. 'Drink?' she asked.

'Am I driving?' I asked back. Daring again, you see.

'I don't know yet.'

'I'll chance it,' I said. 'Got any gin?'

'Is the Pope Catholic?'

It was a bit like ping-pong.

'Tonic?' she asked. 'Lime or vermouth?' The perfect hostess.

'Tonic will be fine.'

'Put on some music. I won't be a second.'

'Anything in particular?'

'You choose.'

She had something for just about everybody. And something by just about everybody. I chose Van Morrison. She had every album he'd done, I think. I went for *Into the Music*. It's one of my favourites.

'Good choice,' she said when she came back with two tumblers that could comfortably have accommodated a family of goldfish each. I almost rolled over on my back and let her tickle my tummy when she said that. Almost, not quite. My willpower was strong. So was the gin and tonic. But unfortunately I've discovered that the stronger the gin, the weaker the will becomes.

We drank two cocktails each. I was starting to get a buzz and she was looking better by the minute. At twenty to eight I said, 'Want to go?'

'Sure, I'll get my coat.' She put her glass on one of the shelves and left the room. She was gone less than a minute. When she came back she was wearing a white mink coat of such an old-fashioned cut that it was bang up-to-date. She saw me looking at it. 'What's the matter?' she asked.

'Nothing,' I said. 'You don't see coats like that much any more.'

'Are you a conservationist?'

'I keep a cat,' I replied.

'My grandmother bought this coat on Fifth Avenue in 1948,' she said. 'These little suckers would have been dead by now anyway.'

'Fine,' I said. 'But aren't you worried that someone from the Animal Liberation Front is going to take offence and spray paint on it?'

'If some pink-haired little shit even tries, I'll Mace the motherfucker,' she hissed, and opened her handbag. Right on top was a tear gas spray. I stepped back and raised my hands in surrender.

'I believe you,' I said. 'I eat meat myself.'

She grinned. 'Me too. Let's go and eat some.'

We went out into the street together. She spotted my car right away. 'Is that yours?'

I nodded.

'I might have guessed,' she said. 'Penis substitute.'

You should know if anyone does, I thought, but said nothing. Just smiled. What the fuck? I was enjoying myself.

The restaurant was in the King's Road. It was on three levels. The floors were pink opaque plastic with covered lights actually set in them, like at the bottom of a swimming pool. The stairs were made of polished chrome. The tables were made of more chrome, with pink tablecloths. The front window was huge and gave a clear view in and out to the street. All in all it was like eating on stage.

We got a table on the top level where we had a great view of the rest of the restaurant and the tops of passing vehicles outside. We had three waiters. It was so crowded round our table I felt as if we were in the middle of a rugby scrum. It was one of those places where only the person who the head waiter thinks is paying the bill gets a menu with prices listed. For what they were asking for a steak sandwich you could buy a whole cow in my local butcher.

Juanita loved every minute of it and every ounce of attention. I hadn't been surrounded by so many solicitous people since the last time I was on an operating table, and it made me a bit edgy. We ordered two Bloody Marys. It thinned out the crowd a little and gave us some room to breathe.

'We'll order when we've got our drinks,' I said.

'Of course,' said the head waiter, and stalked off to worry someone else. The last of the trio popped our napkins on to our laps, smiled, then saw another party at the door and headed off in their direction.

'Thank Christ for that,' I said.

'You get used to it,' said Juanita. 'When you spend as much money as you're going to spend tonight, they think you deserve some attention.'

Just then the Bloody Marys arrived. There was so much foliage in the glasses I was worried about snipers. The drinks waiter stood for a moment until I tasted the aperitif. It was perfect and I told him so. He blushed and backed away, then turned and trotted down the stairs to the bar.

'See,' said Juanita. 'Alone at last.'

'What do you want to eat?' I asked.

She studied her menu and I studied mine. There was something from every sub-continent listed. 'What do you think?' she asked.

'I don't mind,' I said. I really didn't. I was quite content to sit looking at her all evening and chew on a dry crust and drink tap water. Though even that would have cost me twenty-five nicker.

'Avocado salad to start, if the avocado's edible. Soft-shell crab to follow, with stir-fried vegetables and angel's hair noodles.'

I went for gazpacho, duck with mangetout in oyster sauce and fried rice with lobster. The head waiter was at my shoulder, his notebook at the ready, as I closed the menu. After some discussion on the flavour and ripeness of the avocado pear he took our order. The wine waiter was hovering in the wings and suggested a white Burgundy. I took his advice.

When we were once more alone, Juanita lit up a Marlboro and sat back in her seat and sipped at her Bloody Mary. 'Why'd you phone me?' she asked.

'I wanted to see you again.'

'Why? I wasn't exactly wonderful to you the last time we met.'

I shrugged. 'Why not?'

'My favourite two words in the English language,' she said. 'Are we going to be friends?'

'I don't know,' I said. 'But we might be.

'Just don't expect too much from me. I tend to let people down if they do that.'

'I'll remember,' I said.

I think you can tell a lot about a person by going out to eat with them. I like people who share their food. Mainly because whatever I order, everything else on the table always looks better. Juanita was a sharer. She wanted to taste my soup and insisted I try her salad. When the main courses arrived we left the dishes in the middle and just dived in where we wanted. Her crab was excellent, although a little messy to eat, and we had to call for another finger bowl.

We ate everything and didn't care how greasy we got, and by the time we'd finished I thought that, yes, we were going to end up friends, if not more than that. The food was excellent. The wine was as good as the waiter had said, and the bottles kept coming. For dessert she had lemon sorbet. I passed. By ten-thirty we'd finished our meal and were sitting over wicked little cups of espresso coffee and Sambuca. I was too drunk to drive and wondered where I'd end up resting my head. Juanita was smoking her fifteenth Marlboro of the evening and rabbiting away about some author of hers who was trying to get her into bed. Two minds with but a single thought.

'You're not listening,' she said. 'Am I beginning to bore you already?'

'No,' I replied. 'I was wondering, if I left my car on the yellow line outside your place and got a cab home, would it still be there in the morning, or towed away or clamped or what?'

'A bit pissed, are we?'

'I have been soberer. More sober,' I said.

She grinned a wicked grin. 'You are too, aren't you? So do I send you home or do I not?'

'You tell me,' I said. I'd already realised that if she was in the mood to tease, nothing I could say or do, short of gagging her, would stop her.

'Do you want to go on somewhere?' she asked. 'Or do you want to come back to my place for a nightcap?'

'I don't care,' I said.

'We could go dancing,' she said. 'But maybe another time. Perhaps we should talk.'

'Perhaps we should,' I said. 'I'll get the bill.'

I caught the eye of one of our waiters and he brought a little leather folder with the bill tucked securely inside. I looked at it. Not bad. Not bad compared to the price of a new BMW. But for a meal for two, possibly a little steep. I paid for it on Access, and to hell with it.

The waiter brought Juanita's coat and helped her on with it. We wished our waiting team good night and left. It was getting chilly outside, and she slid her arm into mine and we walked back to her place, our bodies touching.

I stood in the entry as she fumbled her keys into the locks. I looked at the back of her hair, almost white in the darkness of the doorway as it flowed over the collar of her white coat. She looked like a ghost in front of me. I touched her shoulder just to make sure she was real.

'What?' she said.

'Nothing,' I said back. 'Just making sure you were there.'

'You're strange, Nick. You know that?'

She pushed the door open, and went into the hall and switched on the light. I went in after her, and pushed the door closed behind me and followed her to the sitting room. She switched on the spots and spun the dimmer until they were just a pink glow in the ceiling. She went to the CD player and punched it on. She selected a disc and slipped it into the jaws of the machine and adjusted the volume. I knew the album well. Ray Charles and Milt Jackson, *Soul Meeting*. A piano and vibes instrumental duet. I didn't even know it had been released on compact disc. The music was sweet and mellow, and filled the room like cool water.

'Want a drink?' she asked.

'Sure.'

'Brandy?'

'Sounds good.'

'I'll be just a minute,' she said, and left the room. She shrugged off her coat as she went. I sat on the sofa and let the music wash me clean. I didn't know why I was there. I was cheating on Fiona. I hadn't cheated on anyone for years. I knew that we were finished, but still it made me feel sad. I wondered what I was starting in its place. Maybe nothing. Maybe something. I fumbled a cigarette out of its packet and lit it.

Juanita came back with two balloon glasses and a bottle of brandy that was older than both of us put together. She poured a slug into each glass. I took mine from her and warmed it between my palms. The smoke from the cigarette between my fingers rippled as I moved my hands.

'What am I doing here?' I asked.

'I don't know.'

'Nor do I.'

'But I'm glad you are.'

'My daughter is coming to visit tomorrow,' I said.

'Do you see her often?'

'Not as often as I'd like to. My wife – my *ex*-wife,' I corrected myself, 'doesn't really approve of me.'

'I wonder why that is?' said Juanita. And we looked at each other and laughed.

'If your daughter's coming tomorrow, do you want to go?' she asked.

I lifted the brandy glass and looked at her through it. I shook my head. 'She's not coming until after school. That's a lifetime away.'

'What do you want to do then?' she said. If she expected me to say 'fuck', she was wrong.

'Talk,' I said. 'Let's talk, like we said we'd do. We've got good booze. Good music. The place is warm. Let's talk for a while.'

'What about?'

'You,' I said. 'You know about me from Wanda. Let's talk about you.'

So we talked, or rather she did. She told me that her parents were dead. That the house belonged to her, and she collected the rent for the other two flats in the building. She told me her mother and father had left her enough money so that she didn't have to work, but that she enjoyed the publishing game. She told me she was twenty-five, but it was hard to believe. She said she'd just come out of a long affair with a man she thought she'd marry, but he'd had other ideas. She told me that she was feeling very vulnerable when she'd met me at Wanda's funeral.

I said that the queue formed on the right. That sometimes I felt so vulnerable that it was like I had an army of ants under the skin on my shoulders. She said she knew the feeling.

We made love on the sofa, and drank neat brandy from the bottle as we did it. At one point she started to cry, and I felt her tears falling on my chest like rain drops. I pulled her down close

converted, anonymous nineties model that you could never find in a supermarket car park.

We caught a 68 to the Aldwych and walked up to Covent Garden. It gets less and less like London every time I go there, and more and more like some bastardized mix of Venice and Greenwich Village, New York.

I hate buskers and fucking street theatre, always have done. I think my mum must have been frightened by a mime artist when she was pregnant.

Judith, of course, loves it. But then she loves MTV, so what do you expect?

I was glad I'd left the car at home. If I was going to get through the day I was going to need a drink or three. But no pubs. I'd got that message.

Luckily Covent Garden is full of cafés that serve alcohol. By eleven-fifteen we were sitting on uncomfortable white plastic chairs outside one. Judith was drinking orange juice and chewing on a pastry. I was on my second glass of white wine and watching the world go by.

Judith had already conned me out of ten quids' worth of violently coloured writing paper and envelopes and a fistful of felt tip pens. 'I have to write to my friends at school,' she informed me darkly. 'Sometimes they don't believe that Louis isn't my real daddy.'

I pondered that one as I sipped my wine. Was it a good or a bad thing?

When the pastry and the juice were gone and she'd talked me out of another glass of wine, we got down to the serious business of the day. I won't list the shops we went to. They were too many and various for that. All I knew was that by one o'clock I'd done a great deal of hard cash in cold blood, and was loaded down with all sorts of carrier bags and parcels. I was also beginning to realise that Judith was growing up fast and getting more sophisticated in her tastes. Once again I didn't know if that was a good or a bad thing.

McDonald's was out. Instead she chose Ed's Diner for lunch. It was the 'in' place, she told me. I wasn't about to argue. At least Ed's was licensed and served good burgers too. We demolished four with cheese between us, and pie and ice-cream for dessert. Judith plumped for a chocolate milk shake and I drank pale American beer and looked down Old Compton Street at the mess they'd made of Soho. Most of the strip joints and mysterious drinking clubs I'd known when I was on the force had vanished, to be replaced by T-shirt shops and expensive restaurants. Christ, some days you do realise that you're getting old.

After lunch we caught the 2.15 showing of the latest teenage hit movie in a cinema in Leicester Square where I felt like the only male in the place old enough to shave, and after we cabbed over to Selfridge's to meet Fiona, and got there by quarter past four.

She was sitting at a table in the coffee bar and Judith went charging over to sit with her while I queued up for some more food. That's another thing you forget about kids. No matter what time of day or night it is, they always seem to be hungry.

I sat and drank coffee whilst Judith ate two coffee cream eclairs and scarfed up Orangina, and she and Fiona rattled on about the shops they were going to visit the next week. Fiona looked stunning, and I felt guilty again about Juanita O'Caine, and horny for both of them, and got depressed. Neither of my companions noticed.

We sat there until the shop shut whilst the pair of them chewed the fat. I was redundant, but they were so animated and enthusiastic about life that I soon cheered up again. When it came near to closing time they decided they wanted to go window shopping. I pretended I didn't, but let them talk me round. We dumped Judith's parcels in the back of Fiona's new car. It was just what I'd expected: red, shiny, teardrop-shaped, loaded with extras, and about as individual as a toilet seat. She seemed to like it though, and whipped it out of the car park and found a parking space near Bond Street in her usual fashion.

The three of us walked down to Piccadilly and back up Regent Street. It was like having a family again. I held both their hands and we dawdled along looking in the shop windows and spending money we didn't have.

About eight we went to a Chinese restaurant in Maddox Street, full of American tourists with prices to match. What the hell? Access could bear it, even if I couldn't.

Fiona drove us home and dropped us off. Judith was asleep in the back of the car and I carried her upstairs. She came to long enough to wash her face, clean her teeth and put on her nightie. She was so tired she even refused a biscuit and a glass of milk. She went straight to bed with Cat and I watched the late movie with the volume down so as not to disturb her.

25

Sunday was peaceful. Judith was up early, and out of the bathroom and dressed by nine. I lay in bed and watched her as she fed Cat. He gave me the kind of look that said he could get used to that sort of service. I gave him the kind of look back which said he shouldn't bother.

Judith brought me tea in bed. Now I knew how Cat felt. She turned on the TV, and *He-Man* got me up and into the bathroom. Once dressed I went and got the papers while she cooked me a full English breakfast. I was a bit worried, but it was exactly how I liked it. Something her mother had never managed in all the years we were married.

Judith just had cereal and, as I attacked my bacon and eggs, dwelt relentlessly and ghoulishly on the dangers of cholesterol on a man of my age. I told you she was growing up.

We read as we ate, and she lapped up the *News of the Screws*, which her mother wouldn't let in the house. We made a pact to tell no tales about what we did whilst she was staying with me. After breakfast we stacked the dishes in the sink, and it was time for the crosswords. Whilst I was wrestling with three across in the Everyman, Judith got on the dog and bone, as she insisted on calling it, and spoke to Fiona. She did Telecom a favour and talked until I was on fourteen down. I wasn't really listening, but heard talk of a return to Bond Street. I shook my head sadly.

When she hung up, she informed me we were going to lunch with Fiona at a Mexican restaurant off Shaftesbury Avenue. I went and checked the Alka-Seltzer situation.

Fiona picked us up in the Passat about twelve. She was totally in love with the thing, and wouldn't go in anything else. She showed off at every set of lights, burning off everything else on the road. If you get what I mean. All the boy racers tried to take her on, but they might as well have stayed in bed. With her window wound down and her long black hair flying in the breeze, they didn't stand a chance.

We were parked and sitting outside a boozer in one of the tiny streets on the edge of Soho, me with my first overpriced imported lager of the day in front of me, by twelve twenty-five.

It was just as well I hadn't driven as I got a bit Brahmsed on Margaritas again at lunch. Over the coffee Judith informed me she was spending the whole of the next day and night with Fiona. Shopping, then a sort of pyjama party at Fiona's flat. It was going to be all girls together. That suited me down to the ground. I had other fish to fry.

'Fine,' I said to Judith. 'I'll get you some cash on the way home. I'm not going to have Fiona spending all her pennies on you.'

Fiona pulled a face. So did Judith.

'What are you going to do, Daddy?' asked Judith.

'I'll find something to occupy the time, Princess.'

A slow drive out in the country in the direction of East Grinstead, I thought.

'I've got a shoot early Tuesday,' said Fiona. 'Can you come round for Judith?'

'What time?'

'I've got to be out by seven.'

'No problem.'

'I'll cook you breakfast,' said Judith.

'Suits me. But you'd better get something in. Last time I was round there all I got was cold pizza.'

Fiona pulled another face. It was almost like old times. Almost, but not quite.

We went on the river in the afternoon. It was warm and pleasant, and I was asleep before we got to Chelsea Harbour. When the cruise was over, Fiona took us back to mine, and we played Trivial Pursuit, and let Judith win, and got a take-out pizza and a video. Fiona went home about eleven and promised to pick up Judith the next morning at ten.

She was as good as her word and turned up in her new car right on the dot. I kissed them both goodbye. Told them I hoped they had a good time and didn't spend too much of my money, and that I'd see them both early the next day.

After they were safely away, I got into the car and dug my book of maps out of the glove compartment. I found the village near Kellerman's cottage right away. I guessed it would take about ninety minutes to get there.

I'd guessed right. I followed Natalie's instructions after I came off the A22 at East Grinstead, and found the place easily.

The cottage was down a secluded lane off the B2110, a quiet road between Forest Row and Hartfield on the edge of the Ashdown Forest.

It was surrounded by a picket fence that had once been white, next to a field that had once been part of an orchard. In the field, stumpy trees were trying hard to grow stunted fruit but they were fighting a losing battle against what looked like a generation of neglect.

I parked the car out of sight of the road. There was a light breeze and clouds moved across the face of the sun, making the day alternately bright and dark. The cottage looked desolate enough in the sunshine but, when the sun disappeared and the breeze blew cold, it looked like a place I'd sooner be leaving rather than arriving at. The front path was thick with old leaves and bits of branches from last winter's storms.

I pushed open the gate and walked up to the porch. The windows were filthy and part of the guttering under the roof at one side of the house had collapsed, and the brick was stained green with rainwater. I unlocked the front door and pushed it open. It caught on a mountain of mail, and I pushed hard, and squeezed through the gap, and shut the door behind me.

The house was deadly silent. No clock ticking. No sound of traffic from outside. No birds in the trees in the field, not even an aeroplane in the sky. Silence filled the hall and I could almost hear my own heart beating. I knelt down and collected the letters into a big pile and went through them. The earliest postmark I could find was the previous February, which fitted. There was nothing addressed to David Kellerman. Anything that wasn't addressed to 'The Occupier' was addressed to Donald King. David Kellerman. Donald King. D. K. The same initials. The oldest trick in the book.

But why did he need a fake name if all he was doing was leaving the family home and setting up a love nest with his girlfriend? I was beginning to think that Robber, for all his shortcomings, had been right. He was an old thief taker after all. When he'd said that Kellerman was dirty, it looked like he'd been right. And I remembered that he'd said that James Webb was dirty too.

Amongst the mail were poll tax demands, telephone bills from blue through red, and a card saying that the phone would be cut off if the bill wasn't paid. That was dated the previous June. There were also demands from the electricity company. When I tried the light switch in the hall, the power was off.

I went through the house from top to bottom. The hallway had two inside doors, and a staircase going upwards. The door on the left led to a kitchen. It was tidy but smelled stale and there was dust on all the surfaces. The sink was dry and empty. There was a half glass door leading on to a path at the side of the house where the dustbins were kept. It was locked and the key was missing. Another door led down into the cellar. It was pitch dark inside, and I went out to the car and got my flashlight.

I shone it into the cellar, down a flight of five or six wooden steps. The cellar ran the whole length and width of the house and looked empty. I didn't go down. I turned off the flashlight and went back into the hall, and towards the door at the end. It opened into a living room. The room was furnished with a comfortable-looking three-piece suite, a dining table, four upright chairs, a low coffee table between the sofa and an open fireplace of red brick which about filled the wall on my right. The fireplace was empty except for cold ashes.

The wall opposite the fireplace was lined with bookcases. There were a few books on the shelves. Ruth Rendell. Agatha Christie. Jilly Cooper. On the middle shelf was the phone. It was dead. Next to it was a tray loaded with bottles of spirits and dusty glasses and an empty ice bucket. Opposite me, behind long curtains, were French windows leading on to a crazy paved rectangle with tufts of tough-looking crab grass sprouting through the cement between the paving stones. Encroaching on to the patio was the wilderness that had probably once been a neat back garden. Now the lawn and flower beds had run wild.

I went upstairs. There was a landing at the top. Again, there were two closed doors. The one at the head of the stairs led into the bathroom, and the other into the only bedroom. I searched the bedroom first. There was a large double bed, neatly made. Two bedside cabinets, a free-standing wardrobe, a chest of drawers, a dressing table with triple mirrors, a couple of chairs, and that was it. But it was expensive stuff and all new. I suppose Kellerman got a discount, being sort of in the trade.

In the ceiling was a trap door. I pulled one of the chairs underneath it, and pushed the door up and open. There was a ladder in the loft and I tugged it down, got off the chair and climbed up the ladder, and stuck my head through the trap. Just roof space. Empty. I could see pinpricks of light through the roof tiles. It looked filthy, so I left it and climbed down.

I went through everything in the bedroom. In the wardrobe a woollen dress, size twelve, from Fenwick's; a man's suit, size 40 regular. A blue overcoat, same size. Both with Harrods labels. Three white shirts on hangers and a floral tie looped around a coat hanger. In the bottom of the wardrobe was a pair of Paul Smith loafers, size nine. I went through the pockets of the clothes. Empty. The chest of drawers held a couple of men's sweaters and some underwear, cotton from Jermyn Street. There was women's underwear, too. Sexy, from Bond Street. I thought about Natalie Hooper sitting in her wheelchair back in her bungalow in Epsom, and I must admit I did wonder.

The dressing table held make up, skin cleanser, perfume, tissues, cotton wool balls, earrings and a silver bracelet. Just what you'd expect if you'd ever lived with a woman. All the cosmetics were top of the range. The perfume Christian Dior and Chanel. The bedside cabinets were empty except for another Agatha Christie paperback in one drawer. I checked the carpet. Good quality Wilton, beautifully fitted. I tore it up around the edges. Nothing. Finally I looked underneath the mattress. Not even a bed bug.

I went along the hall to the bathroom. It smelled stale, like the kitchen. The flannels and towels were bone dry and there were spiders in the bath. I checked the medicine cabinet. The usual. Two dry toothbrushes in a glass. Toothpaste, shampoo, mouthwash, soap, aspirin. I pulled the siding away from the bath. Just a dead mouse. I left it in peace. I pulled up the carpet on the landing, stairs and in the hall. Zip.

I went back into the kitchen and checked the drawers there. Nothing special. I went through the food cartons and emptied the flour and sugar jars and checked the fridge. Something had gone badly off. I checked the salad crisper and the ice compartment.

Just the remains of a lettuce that had gone beyond vegetable state, and a dry ice tray.

This time I went down into the cellar. As I had thought, it was totally empty. The floor was solid concrete.

I was getting bored.

I went back into the sitting room and searched it, and pulled up the carpet there too. Nothing again. I unbolted the French windows and went into the garden. I found a path through the wilderness that I followed until I came to a large shed. The door was unlocked. I went inside and got a bit lucky. The shed held a small generator. It was switched off. Next to it was a five-gallon drum of petrol.

I checked the generator's tank. It was almost full. I found the ignition and started it up. Now, at least, there should be light in the cottage.

The walls of the shed were lined with shelves stacked with boxes of nuts and bolts and nails and screws separated by size. There were two power drills, and enough tools to stock Halford's, all lightly oiled and gleaming, through a layer of dust, on neatly labelled hooks screwed into the walls. It was lucky the place hadn't been robbed in all the time it had stood empty. Apart from the generator the shed gave me nothing.

I went back out into the garden and smoked a cigarette and thought a bit. Natalie had told me the deeds to the house were *in* the house, but they weren't. At least, not as far as I could see, and I'd searched pretty thoroughly. And believe me I've had practice. Normally I'd say they weren't there, and leave it at that. But there weren't any papers at all. Nothing. Now I knew Kellerman had been leading some sort of weird double existence so there had to be something, somewhere, that referred to the Donald King part of his life that he couldn't take home or leave at his office. And obviously nothing had turned up yet.

The police must have gone through everything that they could get their hands on with the proverbial fine toothcomb.

There was obviously no documentation elsewhere that the cottage existed or else someone would have turned up before me. Plus the house in Crown Point had been broken into and searched thoroughly by some third party long after the murder had taken place and the police had left. So someone else knew, or thought they knew, that there was *something* to find. The people who had been following me obviously, the people who had killed McKilkenney. But what? Not just the deeds to the cottage surely? Why would anyone be bothered with them? The place belonged to James Webb free and clear as far as I could see, even if Kellerman was calling himself Father Christmas. And it was clear Webb knew nothing about it or else he'd have come forward with a claim.

There had to be something here. Unless Kellerman had taken the papers outside and buried them, or he'd rented a safety deposit box, or lodged them at some tame solicitor under his fake name, they were inside. I lit another cigarette and looked back at the house. It sat four square and mysterious. There *was* something there, I was sure of it. There just had to be.

I went back for a closer look at the attic and cellar. I went upstairs again, removed my jacket and climbed the ladder once more. The roof space was totally empty, and the insulation between the rafters was old and hadn't been disturbed for years. I went back down the ladder, collected my jacket and returned to the kitchen. I was thirsty. I opened the fridge, which had started working again, and found a can of diet Pepsi in the cooler. I opened the top and took a swallow, then went into the sitting room and topped up the can from the bottle of vodka on the bookcase. I smoked another cigarette and finished the can. It was well after three by the time I went down to the cellar again.

In the harsh electric light it looked even emptier than before, if that makes sense. The walls were made of white plaster, out of which the brick legs of the foundations protruded about four inches, so the walls looked something like a Zebra crossing on its edge. Three or four feet of grubby white, then two feet of dark brick, then white again, all round the room. I went round with the end of my torch, tapping all the walls. They looked and felt solid enough, so that was that. No joy.

I went back upstairs again and sat with the bottle of vodka and a lot of bad thoughts. I was tired and dirty and it seemed like I'd wasted another day. I looked out of the filthy windows and watched the afternoon gradually slide into evening. Eventually I finished what was left of the bottle and tossed it into the fireplace with the rest of the ashes.

Then I left. Locked up the cottage and drove back to town. I went straight to my local bar and took a chance on a bowl of chilli washed down with a few beers.

Before I knew it, it was closing time and I got swept out with the rest of the riff-raff.

By the time I got home it was nearly midnight. Cat was waiting on the front step and gave me a good telling off for abandoning him for the day. I let him in, fed him, and called Fiona. She answered right away.

It was good to hear her voice. And Judith's. Like life could be normal, and not everyone was bent. I told Judith she should have been in bed long ago.

She said that she was. Watching TV. I was too pleased to hear her to argue. She told me she'd had a great day out with Fiona. I told her I was glad. I didn't tell her where I'd been. Then I told her that I loved her, wished her good night, and sent my love to Fiona.

Judith wished me good night too, and told me that she loved me and would have my breakfast ready at seven sharp. We said goodbye and I waited for her to hang up before I did. It's something that I do.

By that time my head was aching like a bastard. I undressed and got into bed. I lay there for an hour or more, thinking and making my headache worse. I knew there was something wrong with that cottage, but I couldn't figure out what it was. I suppose eventually I fell asleep.

26

26

I wasn't asleep long. The illuminated digital numbers on my bedside clock read 5.35 when I woke up. At least my headache had gone.

I got up and showered. Cat was hungry again. In a lot of ways he reminded me of Judith. I fed the little fucker and kicked him out into the street. Then I went back upstairs and made a mug of Typhoo with too much sugar that I drank while I was getting dressed. I put on a denim shirt, jeans and my favourite scuffed-up pair of old Doc Marten's eleven holers. By that time it was past six and I went down to the car and took a slow drive to The Oval where I had been assured breakfast would be waiting. I smoked the first cigarette of the day as I steered through the quiet streets. But all the time I was thinking about the cottage in East Grinstead and the secrets I knew it hid.

Judith answered the flat door and I could smell bacon cooking as I followed her upstairs. Fiona must have taken my advice and got some supplies in. We went straight into the kitchen. Fiona wasn't about.

'I knew you'd be early,' said Judith. 'So I was too.'

'Good girl,' I said. 'Been having fun?'

'Terrific,' she replied. 'But I haven't spent much money.'

'I'm glad to hear it.'

'Yet.'

Fiona must have been giving her a few tips.

Then I heard footsteps on the stairs and Fiona came into the kitchen, dressed and ready to go out to work.

It never ceased to amaze me that, when she went out to one of her shoots, she looked positively plain. If she ever could. Her hair was up in big bendy rollers under a scarf and her face was totally devoid of make up. She was bundled up in a huge leather flying jacket and leggings.

'Hi, beautiful,' I said.

'Don't. I look like a fright.'

'You look OK to me. Good enough to eat, almost.'

'Better than my bacon?' interrupted Judith.

'Nothing looks better than that.'

'Do you want anything, Fiona?' asked the chef.

'Oh, no. It's too early. I'd better go.'

'No coffee?' asked Judith solicitously.

'No. I'll puke if I do. I'll feel better when I get some air.' She kissed us both and left. 'I'll be back by lunchtime,' she said. 'Give me a ring and we'll do something.'

'Good,' said Judith. I flipped her a wave and Fiona left.

Judith dished up the sandwiches and tea.

'So what are we going to do this morning, kid?' I asked.

'I think we should stop calling me kid for a start,' she replied tartly.

I looked at her. She reminded me of her mother when we first met. When I fell for her. 'OK,' I said. 'We'll knock the "kid" bit on the head. So what shall we do?'

'Can we go shopping?'

'Sure. Where? The West End?'

'How about somewhere around here? I was in the West End yesterday.'

'What do you want to buy?'

'Clothes?'

'What, more clothes?'

'I hardly bought anything yesterday. Just some T-shirts and my new jeans you haven't noticed I'm wearing.'

I must admit I hadn't. I had a lot on my mind. 'Sorry, darling,' I said. 'I was too distracted by your natural beauty to see them.' She blushed, but I knew she liked it. 'There's not much choice locally,' I said.

'What about Croydon?'

'You want to go to Croydon?' I said in disbelief. As far as I was concerned it was a bit like saying you wanted to go to Middlesbrough.

'It's supposed to be good. Some of the girls at school told me.'

'All right then. Croydon it is.'

We got ourselves together and went out to the car and I drove south. She was full of chatter as we went. 'Do you think if I asked Fiona she'd let me go to work with her one day?' she said.

'On a shoot?'

'Yes.'

'It's a thought,' I said. 'You really want to go?'

'Yes.'

Christ, I could imagine her mother's face. 'I suppose so,' I said. 'But you'd have to promise to keep your training bra on.' She looked as shocked as only a ten-year-old, going on eleven, can. Then she covered her mouth and laughed. So did I. Except I didn't cover my mouth.

So far it had been a good morning.

It was about to change. For the worse.

I'd been following the main roads, and when I got close to Beulah Hill I looked in the mirror and saw a car coming up fast behind me with its headlights on full beam. I thought it was the law on the way to a shout and slowed down and pulled off the crown of the road. But it wasn't police. It was an old blue Volvo, battered and scarred with rust. It pulled past me then cut in, and I saw smoke from its tyres as it braked. I slammed on *my* brakes so hard that my seat belt cut painfully into my shoulder. The front of the car dipped and I heard the sound of metal on the roadway. The Jaguar slewed into the middle of the road and stalled.

'Arsehole!' I said, and opened the door to get out. Then both front doors of the Volvo opened. Two men got out and came running back towards us. The driver was huge. Blubbery, with short hair the colour of carpet dust, wearing a nylon windbreaker and jeans. He was carrying a pump-action shotgun. The other man was much younger, wearing a single-breasted tan mackintosh. He was empty-handed.

The driver screamed: 'Get out of the car. Both of you.'

I looked at Judith. She looked as scared as I felt.

Then the driver was at my door. He ripped it open and stuck the barrel of the gun in my face. 'Out, you bastard. Out. Out. Out. Get the kid,' he shouted at his mate.

I did as I was told and the passenger opened Judith's door and dragged her out too. 'Don't!' I said, and the geezer with the gun whacked me round the head with the barrel. Not hard enough to knock me out, but hard enough to hurt.

He stuck the muzzle of the shotgun back into my face. So close that I could smell metal and gun oil. 'Where is it?' screamed the driver at the top of his lungs. I noticed that other cars were stopping and people were getting out to see what was happening, and a little knot of pedestrians had gathered. But, wisely, well out of range.

'What?' I said.

'What she told you about.'

'Who?'

'The fucking cripple, you cunt. Where is it?'

Natalie.

'I don't know...'

He hit me again. In the ribs this time. So hard I couldn't speak. 'We'll kill the kid,' he screamed.

I looked at him and I knew that if I survived the next few minutes I was going to do for him eventually. We stood like that for a few seconds that seemed like hours, then he pointed the gun at the bonnet of the Jaguar and fired. The shock from the blast shook the car and the windscreen imploded. Someone in the crowd screamed and suddenly a white Rover squad car with blue lights flashing overtook the queue of traffic that had formed behind us and sped along the white line in the middle of the road.

'Fuck!' shouted the driver, pumped the action of the shotgun and fired at the police car. It skidded to a halt and the gunman ran towards it, firing again. The passenger from the Volvo let go of Judith and ran after the driver.

'In the car,' I shouted. My head and gut hurt, but I'd survive. 'Quick, Judith, get in.'

She did as she was told and I slid behind the wheel and hit the ignition. The front seats were covered with pieces of laminated glass, but we both ignored the discomfort. The V-12 engine caught first time. I slammed the car into gear and took off with a scream from the drive wheels. I pulled out past the Volvo and took off in the direction of Beulah Hill. I turned left by the TV mast and took the first side road I saw, cutting through the back doubles towards Upper Norwood. Judith sat white-faced next to me.

'Are you all right?' I said. Christ, let her be all right, I thought.

'Daddy, what happened?' she said. Her lips were white and I knew she was going into shock. I stopped the car, leant over and reached for her. She clung to me tight. She was shaking but unhurt.

'You'll be all right,' I said. 'You'll be all right.' But I was cold with fear for her. Those bastards were going to pay for that fear.

I looked behind me but the street was clear. I sat back and breathed deeply. My ribs felt like they were broken, but I doubted that they were. I looked in the mirror at my head where the gunman had hit me. There was some blood in my hair, but nothing too serious by the looks of it. Too bad if it was.

'Did they hurt you, Daddy?'

'They tried their best.'

'Will you be all right?'

'I'll live,' I said. 'Just so's you have to look after me in my old age.'

She smiled despite herself. She thought that I was joking, but she was probably the only one who would.

I drove straight to my pal Charlie's garage in West Norwood. He runs a legit car sales, servicing, mechanical breakdown and crash repair business behind the High Street there. I've often suspected that it's a chop shop on the quiet but never liked to ask. He looks after my cars for me. Always has. In fact, it was him that rebuilt the E-Type when I first got it cheap while I was in the job. Currently he was storing a Pontiac Trans-Am for me and I needed some wheels with all round glass to drive. I took the Jaguar directly into the yard at the back of the premises and parked close to the body shop.

Charlie spotted me from his office window and came out to see what was occurring. He took one look at the car and shook his head sadly. 'What *have* you been up to now?'

'I fancied some fresh air.'

'Sure you did,' said Charlie.

I got out of the car. My legs were still shaking. Judith got out too and I put my arm around her. 'You remember my daughter Judith,' I said.

'Course I do. Hello, Judith pet. My, but you're getting big.'

Judith put on a brave smile, but said nothing. I squeezed her tight.

'You're not doing too bad yourself,' I said, referring to the paunch which Charlie's smart double-breasted was doing its best to disguise. 'Too many business lunches?'

'Don't change the subject, Nick.' He touched the holes in the bonnet of the Jaguar. 'What the hell's been going on?'

'Metal fatigue,' I said.

He shook his head again. 'Better not let Talulah see it.'

Talulah was the mechanic who actually worked on my cars. She was young and fierce, and took no nonsense from men. The way she acted, you'd think that she owned the cars, and grudgingly loaned them to me.

'Is she about?' I asked.

'You're lucky,' he said. 'She's out on a breakdown.'

'Can I leave this for repair?' I touched the roof of the E-Type.

He sighed. 'I'd never hear the end of it if I said no.' I think he was as wary of Talulah as I was.

'It's in a bit of a state anyway. Could do with a complete overhaul.'

'Well you certainly haven't improved the bodywork.'

'I've been thinking about a re-spray. Red would be good.'

'Well, at least it wouldn't show the bloodstains.'

'Funny. I'll take the Tranny.'

'No you won't. The head's off. Valve flutter.'

'Shit,' I said.

'Not in front of the kid,' he said.

Judith scowled at him.

'And talking of heads, what happened to yours?'

'Walked into a door.'

'Not your day.'

'You could say that. Now, have you got anything I can use as a loaner?'

'Sure. But I'm not going to lend you anything decent if it's going to come back in this state. I have got a business to run, you know?'

'So what then?'

'I've got just the thing for you. Over here.' Judith and I followed him round the back of the workshop. Parked against the wall was a dark blue, P-reg, MkI Ford Granada.

'What, this?' I said.

'You're lucky to get anything. Now, remember, there's no MOT. No tax. No insurance. The body's held together with filler but the engine's good for another hundred thousand miles.'

'Haven't you got anything else?' I asked hopefully.

'No. Take it or leave it. And make up your mind quick. I've got work to do.'

I opened the driver's door. Inside it smelled a bit of mildew and the upholstery was threadbare. But at least it was clean. I checked the pedals. The milometer read sixty thousand. A bit optimistic, even for Charlie I thought. The rubber was worn through to the metal on the accelerator. The keys were in the ignition. I sat behind the wheel and started it. The engine caught first time. I let it idle. It didn't seem too bad. The oil pressure was up and the engine was firing on all cylinders. I put it into drive and the gear box took up smoothly.

'Thanks, Charlie. I'll take it,' I said. 'How much?'

'How long?' he asked.

'Who knows?'

'Forget it. I'll chuck it in with the repairs to the Jag.'

'Cheers,' I said.

'But if you wreck it, I'll charge you five hundred quid.'

'Book price?' I asked.

'My book.'

'In you get, Judith, before Uncle Charlie changes his mind,' I said. And before Talulah gets back and gives me a bollocking about the Jag, I thought.

She did as she was told and I wound down the window and shook hands with Charlie through the gap then drove off.

27

I wasn't going home. Not then. It was too dangerous. I drove down to my local bar and parked the Granada round the back out of sight. Judith and I went in by the side door. The place was deserted at that early hour. I sat her at a table at the rear of the restaurant, out of sight of the front windows, and went and bought two cups of cappuccino. I took them and went and sat down with her. 'Are you OK?' I asked. Stupid question. How would the average ten-year-old be after being fired at by some lunatic with a semi-automatic shotgun?

She nodded.

'Good girl,' I said. What other response was there? She could have been killed. And it would have been my fault. I went cold again at the thought of it. 'I've got a couple of phone calls to make. I won't be a minute.' I got some change at the bar and went to the telephone. I had my notebook in the pocket of my leather jacket. I tapped out Natalie Hooper's number. The telephone was off. Not just not being answered like before. No ringing tone. No answerphone message. Just a single tone backed by a wash of static. A small hole in the Telecom system. The operator wasn't much help. The line was out of order. No reason. She'd report it to the engineers. She wasn't even interested when I told her that the phone belonged to a registered disabled person.

But I knew what had happened. As clearly as if I'd been there myself. I should have called the police. Maybe she was hurt. But I doubted it. These guys didn't operate like that. Get in their way and you ended up dead. Unless you were very lucky. I had been so far. Perhaps my luck was about to run out. I suspected Natalie's already had. And if it had, I wanted to be the one to find her. But what had put them on to her at that late date?

I couldn't think about that right then. I had Judith to worry about. I had to get her somewhere safe. And quick. I called Fiona. She wasn't at home. The answerphone was on. I didn't leave a message. There was no point.

Finally I rang James Webb. He answered on the third ring. 'Jim, it's me, Nick Sharman,' I said.

'Hello,' he said. 'Has something happened?'

'Don't ask. I want to see you.'

'When?'

'Now.'

'Why?'

'It's a long story. I don't want to talk about it on the phone.'

'Sounds mysterious.'

'It is. Are you going to be in all morning?'

'All day,' he said.

'I'll see you in a bit then,' I said and hung up.

I thought about phoning Robber then, and thought better of it. I could talk to him anytime. I went back to where Judith was sitting. The colour was beginning to come back into her face. I was proud of her. She was playing with the froth in her coffee but looked up at me as I sat down. Once again she reminded me of her mother when she loved me.

'Hi, babe,' I said.

'What are we going to do?' she asked.

'*I'm* going to see someone.'

She noticed my inflection. 'What about me?'

'I don't know. I've tried to get hold of Fiona, but she's not in. What do you want to do?'

'Go with you.' That's just what Laura would have said under the circumstances. It was getting spooky.

'I don't know, honey. It could be dangerous.' What a stupid thing to say. It already was dangerous.

'I don't care.'

'I do. And Christ knows what your mother would say if she knew.'

'We won't tell her.'

'How about I take you over to Louis's mother's?' I refused to call her Judith's granny. She wasn't. Any more than Louis was her father.

'No, Daddy. She'd lock me up in a cupboard and feed me seedy cake.'

'I'm sure she wouldn't,' I said. But I wasn't. Anyone with a dentist for a son was suspicious in my book.

Judith pondered for a moment. 'Well, maybe not the cupboard. But she'd feed me seedy cake for sure.'

'Why?'

'Because she hates me. She loves Joseph, but she hates me.'

Joseph, if you haven't already guessed, was Laura and Louis's son.

'I'm sure she doesn't,' I said. But I felt a stab of pain for my daughter.

'She does. That's why she wouldn't have me to stay with her. She says I'm like you.'

'She doesn't know me.'

'She's heard enough about you from Mummy.'

'Nothing good, I hope.' Some fat chance.

'I'll say,' she said, and dived so deep into her coffee cup that when she came up for air there was a blob of froth on her nose. People you love do such beautiful things sometimes. I removed the froth with my thumb and sat back and sucked it.

'OK,' I said. 'You can come with me. But you know I could get into terrible trouble for taking you.'

'I told you I wouldn't tell.'

'Drink up then. We're off to see someone.'

'Who?'

'The guy that hired me for a job.'

'Does that mean I'm a detective too now?'

'If you want to be.'

We finished our coffees and went back to the Granada. I turned in the direction of Crystal Palace again. I had James Webb's address on the card he'd given me on the day we'd met. I got Judith to look up the street name in the *A-Z*. She found it right away. It was on the Dulwich border. The expensive side. A wide, tree-lined street of large semis, all with big front gardens and garages attached. Not as flash as Oakfield, but not bad at all.

Webb's place was halfway down on the right. I parked and climbed out. The street was hushed and there wasn't a soul to be seen. 'Come on then, slowcoach,' I said to Judith. 'Let's go and see the man.'

'What man?' she replied, and we were into one of her favourite routines.

'The man with the power.'

'What power?'

'The power of the hoodoo.'

'Hoodoo?' she asked with a big grin creeping across her face, all troubles seemingly forgotten.

'You do,' I said.

'I do what?'

'Remind me of a man.'

'What man?' she shouted. That particular routine could go on all day, and often had when she was younger.

'Come on, dopey,' I said. 'Let's go. This is serious.' But what can you do? I do what? Now she had me at it.

We got out of the car. I took the keys but left it unlocked. Who was going to nick it? The man with the power maybe. We walked up the path together and Judith held my hand. Christ, she *was* only ten.

I rang the doorbell and Webb answered. 'Come in.' He showed us into a big living room on the right of the hallway. There was no sign of his wife. The room was decorated OK. A bit too 'memories of a fortnight on the Costa Del Sol' maybe. But OK. 'This is my daughter,' I said. 'The domestic responsibility I told you about. Judith – Mr Webb.'

'Jim,' he said. She shook hands solemnly. 'Sit down,' he said. We sat down together on the fat cushions of an overstuffed sofa. Jim remained standing.

'What happened to your head?' he asked.

'A slight *contretemps*.'

'I see,' he said, but he obviously didn't. 'Do you want something to drink?'

I looked at Judith. Now she was a detective I half expected her to ask for a Martini cocktail. Gin. Five to one, with an olive. 'Can I have a Coke?' she asked.

'Sure,' said Jim. 'Ice?'

'Yes, please.'

'Nick?'

'Got a beer?'

'Sure,' he said again, and left us alone.

I looked around the room again. 'Nice place,' I said.

Judith wrinkled her nose. 'I think it's yucky.'

'If you say so,' I replied, and wondered if Jim would mind if I smoked. I guessed he would, having given up and all.

Webb came back with a can of Coke, a can of Heineken and two glasses on a tray. He put it on the coffee table. One glass was half full of ice. He poured out the drinks and gave them to us.

'Nothing for you?' I asked.

'I just had some tea,' he said.

Interesting conversation so far, I thought. 'Jim,' I said, 'I've got kind of a problem.'

'What's that?'

'Someone nearly killed us today. Me and my daughter. That was the slight *contretemps* I told you about.'

He went white, and looked at Judith and then back at me.

'What?' he said. 'Who?'

'That's what I'd like to ask you. You see, Jim, every time I get involved with you, bad things happen. You know what I mean?'

He didn't say or do anything in reply.

'So, Jim, who did you tell that I was back on the case?'

He looked bewildered. 'I don't know what you mean.'

'Sure you do. In fact, only you *do* know.'

'Well, I…'

'Relax,' I said. 'Let's go right back to the beginning. You never did tell me who told you about me in the first place.'

'What do you mean?'

'The first day you came to my office, you said I was well known. Who put you on to me?'

'A bloke I know.'

'What bloke?'

'His name's Keogan. Tony Keogan.'

'Doesn't mean a thing to me. Who is he?'

'He did some work for David.'

'What kind of work?' It was like pulling teeth.

'All sorts. Mostly legal.'

'He's a solicitor or something?'

'No. He studied, but he didn't pass his finals.'

'So what exactly does he do?'

'He's an enquiry agent.'

'A detective?'

'Yes.'

'And he put you on to me. And you were passing out grands. Does he have a private income?'

'No. He said it wasn't his line of work.'

'I bet.'

'It's true.'

'What does he look like?' I asked.

'Tall. Blond. Losing his hair.' He touched his own thinning scalp self-consciously. 'He dresses smart. Always suits, overcoats, collar and tie. You know what I mean?'

I nodded. I did. I also knew he wasn't either of the men in the Volvo. 'So does he have an office?' I asked.

'Sure.'

'Where?'

'Penge.'

'Penge. Great,' I said. 'That was where the car was stolen from that followed me a couple of weeks back. The one that...' Then I stopped. I didn't want to mention Stan McKilkenney's murder in front of Judith. She might be tough, but I didn't think she was quite ready for that. 'You know the one I mean,' I said. He nodded.

'So let's go visit Mr Keogan,' I said.

'What, now?'

'Time's a'wasting. You haven't got anything better to do, have you?'

He shook his head.

'We'll take my car,' I said.

So we did. Penge is just a few minutes from Crystal Palace.

Keogan's office was over a betting shop and was even seedier than mine, if that's possible. It was all locked up. I squinted through the half glass door with 'Anthony Keogan – Enquiry Agent' painted on it in peeling letters. There was a pile of mail on the floor.

'Seems like our bird has flown.'

'But I only spoke to him the other day,' said Webb.

'When?'

'Last Friday.'

'Where?'

'We had lunch.'

'How cosy. Whose idea was it?'

'His.'

'And I suppose you talked about the case?'

'Yes. Did I do wrong?'

'Only if you told him about the old boy I spoke to.'

He looked shamefaced.

'You did, didn't you?' I asked.

He nodded.

'Christ, Jim,' I said, 'you shouldn't have done that.' But it was done, and too late to cry over spilt milk.

'Do you know where he lives?'

He shrugged. 'Local. But I don't know the address.'

'Do you have his home phone number?'

'No, just his office. We're not friends. I only really knew him through David.'

'But well enough to have lunch.'

He nodded.

'Let's look in the phone book,' I said. We went outside and found a telephone box with a local directory in one piece. There were just a few Keogans listed. Only one with the initial 'A'. But that was the office we'd just visited. There were none with a 'T'. I took down the few that there were and went back to Webb's house and tried them all. No luck. No one knew a Tony Keogan.

I tried Natalie Hooper's number again, just on the off chance. Still the unobtainable signal. I had to get over there. And quick.

But first I had to make a decision about what to do with Judith.

As usual I made the wrong one.

28

I quickly called Fiona's number again. Luckily she was back. 'I need a favour,' I said.

'What?'

'Somewhere to stay.'

'Why?' The inevitable question.

'Long story. Can we come over and I'll tell you?'

'Are you in trouble again?'

'Could be.'

'You *and* Judith?'

'That's right.'

'What is it this time?'

'Not on the phone. Can we come over or not?'

'I suppose so.' I'd had warmer invitations.

We left Webb's place and drove to The Oval. I parked the Granada at the back of the flats, out of the way, and we went up. Fiona came to the door looking like she'd lost her chance of stardom and found a dead dog's head in the fridge. It was that bad, believe me. We all went upstairs to the living room.

'Can I use the phone?' I asked.

'Tell me what's happened first,' said Fiona.

'Someone nearly killed us this morning,' I said. 'Now can I use the phone or do I have to go down twenty-seven flights of stairs to find a call box that's working?'

'Use the damn phone then!'

Judith was looking from one of us to the other like a spectator at a tennis match. 'Can you look after Judith?' I said.

'Private call, is it?' said Fiona sarcastically.

'Not really. But I think she could use some care.'

'You're her father.'

'Fiona, please.'

'OK,' she said, then to Judith: 'Come down to the kitchen and keep me company. We'll see if we can find you a drink.'

I winked at Judith as they went out. She didn't wink back. Fiona hadn't mentioned the wound on my head. She was the first person who hadn't.

I sat down in the armchair and pulled the phone over. I phoned Robber. He was in as usual. 'Yes?' he said when he answered. I recognised his voice.

'Sharman,' I said.

He didn't bother to say hello. 'Were you in Beulah Hill this morning?' he demanded.

'You heard,' I said.

'I couldn't avoid it. Shots fired at a police vehicle. People could have been killed.'

'You amaze me. One of the shots was fired at my car. If your blokes hadn't come along, the next would have been at me. Or my daughter.'

He was silent. 'Are you all right?' he asked finally.

'So kind of you to ask. Yes, we are. But the car's fucked. *Did* anyone else get hurt?'

'No. No casualties. But it was a damn close thing. Did you know them?'

'No. But I'd know them again.' I described them to Robber. I knew he'd already have dozens of descriptions, but I'd been closest to them, and every bit helps.

'What was it all about?' he asked.

'I'll give you three guesses.'

'The Kellermans?'

'I'm not doing anything else. And shotguns seem to figure large in their MO.' I didn't tell him what the big bloke had said about Natalie. That could come later. If at all. 'So what did happen after the police arrived?' I asked.

'Your mates took a couple of shots at the car. They blew out one of the front tyres. Then they scarpered.'

'Have you found the Volvo?'

'It turned up in Crystal Palace half an hour later.'

'So soon?'

'Someone set it on fire.'

'Empty, I suppose?'

'What do you think?'

'Fine. Listen, Mr Robber, when you were originally conducting the Kellerman enquiry, did you speak to someone called Tony Keogan? He calls himself an enquiry agent. He's got an office in Penge.'

'Rings a bell,' said Robber. 'Got blond hair? Looks like a bloody undertaker?'

'That sounds like him. I think he's involved.'

'Why's that?'

'He put Webb on to me in the first place. Turned down the job himself. Webb's been keeping him up to date with what's been happening. Now this. By his description, he certainly wasn't there this morning. But that doesn't mean he isn't part of it. Oh, and his office is all closed up with no sign of recent occupation.'

'I told you that bugger Webb was dirty.'

'No, I don't think so. I really think he thought that Keogan was trying to help. Have you got a home address for him?'

'It'll be on the computer.'

'Dig it out and give him a spin.'

'Have you got any proof?'

'No. But when did the Met need proof to put the frighteners on a citizen?'

'Don't be cheeky. I'll check him out. But if he is, that means we're looking at at least three targets. Christ, when is this going to end?'

I didn't answer. I didn't know. But I did know that we were looking at a load more grief before it did.

'What are you going to do?' asked Robber, after a moment.

'I've got a few leads to follow up.'

'Like what?'

'I never divulge professional secrets.'

'Sharman!' There was a definite note of warning in his voice.

'Trust me.'

'Are you at home?'

'No.'

'Where?'

'Another professional secret, I'm afraid.'

'I want to see you. Today. Now.' The warning was more pronounced. More like the Robber I knew.

'I'll be in touch,' I said. 'Tony Keogan. Check him out.' And I hung up.

29

I went and found Fiona and Judith in the kitchen downstairs. They were both sitting at the table. Fiona was drinking bottled Steinlager from the neck. Judith had orange juice.

I wasn't offered anything. Fiona looked at me as if I was a plague carrier. Which I suppose I was, in a way.

It didn't bother me. I wasn't staying. 'I've got to go out,' I said.

'Really?' said Fiona. In that icy way that some women have when they're *really* pissed off with you, and just deciding where to put the blade.

'Really,' I replied. 'Can Judith stay with you?'

'Of course she can.' She hesitated. 'You're back on that case, aren't you?'

I nodded.

'Why? After all you said.'

'Who knows?'

'Is that all you can say?'

I nodded again. It was that desperate moment when all bets are off. When everything said in the past – every promise, every vow – becomes worthless. It was over. I knew that nothing could ever be the same between us again. It felt like I'd been hit in the ribs again. But harder.

'Then you'd better go.' She didn't say any more because Judith was there. And thank God for that. Things were bad enough as it was.

I said goodbye, but only Judith acknowledged me. Then I left and drove to Epsom again.

The street full of bungalows was as quiet as the last time I'd been there. I drove to the last house in the row. All the curtains were drawn, and the house looked deserted, but the Mini was still parked outside the garage. The whole thing stunk on ice.

I didn't stop. Just drove past, and right at the end on to a cross street and parked in a turnaround at the end. Construction hadn't reached that far, but foundations were marked out in the mud. I walked back to Natalie's front gate and up to the front door. I rang the bell. No answer. Again I rang. Again no answer.

I took the path that went round to the back of the house. The kitchen door was locked, and the blinds were down over the glass of the door and the kitchen window. I kept going. The curtains were drawn as well over the big sitting room window that looked out over the bare earth of the back garden. I went back to the kitchen door. Being the last house, next to the deserted building site, it wasn't overlooked. I picked up a half brick that formed part of the decoration of the path, protected my eyes with one hand and slammed the brick into the glass half of the door with the other. The glass broke with a crash. I stood still for a minute or two, waiting and listening in case anyone raised the alarm. Nothing.

I rubbed the brick around the edge of the frame to dislodge any loose pieces of glass and reached in. The key was in the lock. I turned it, and then the handle on the outside, and I was in.

The house was dark and silent inside. I shut the door and let up the shade to get some illumination. The place had been turned over. Not carefully. The kitchen had been trashed. I crunched across broken glass and china. The living room had been done too. The phone had been ripped out of the wall, answerphone, junction box and all. The drawers from the cabinet had been emptied and their contents thrown anywhere. All the books had been pulled off the shelves. The usual. I'd seen it before.

I called out her name. My voice echoed through the silence. No answer. I went into the hall. I saw that one of the doors had been kicked in. It led into the bathroom. Natalie was inside. In her wheelchair. Looking at the wall. Dead. She'd slashed one wrist. It had been enough. The single-sided razor blade was still in her other hand. Blood had soaked the carpet around one wheel of the chair in an almost perfect circle. It was brown and crusted. I touched her face. It was like ice.

'Oh, baby, I'm sorry,' I said.

I wondered what she'd told them. Not as much as they wanted to know, I'd bet. Otherwise they wouldn't have come after me and Judith that morning.

She must have done this whilst they were still in the house or else I'd've had to kick the bathroom door down myself. I closed her eyes. Her eyelids were cold and stiff under my fingers. I went and looked at the front door. The bolts and chain were off. There was no sign of a forced entry. She must have known whoever came to the door. Someone from her past. I'd bet my life it was Keogan. Natalie had. I was looking forward more and more to meeting him.

I went back to the kitchen and let myself out through the back door. I smeared my fingers on the handle as I went and threw the brick on to the building site next door.

I didn't notify anyone. There was nothing anyone could do for her. She was going to get ripe over the next few days. Maybe that would alert someone. Or someone would see the back door smashed. She must have visitors sometimes. Apart from me and whoever had made her kill herself.

I wondered what the police would make of it. I couldn't let that be a problem. Someone else was going to have to clean up the mess I'd made. It wouldn't be the first time, and I suspected it wouldn't be the last.

You're right. I behaved like a bastard, leaving her like that. But I wanted to finish it on my own. Bringing in the law then would only muddy the water. They wouldn't care how brave she'd been. I did. And somewhere out in the world people were going to find out just how much.

I walked briskly back down the road. I hoped no one was watching. I got to the car and sat back and breathed deeply. Jesus Christ. Another fuck-up in my brilliant career.

I sat there, and chewed on my bottom lip and tried to figure out what exactly had happened. How had they got to Natalie? How come they were always just one step behind me? I hadn't been followed I was sure. And I hadn't told anyone I'd been to see Natalie Hooper. If they'd trailed me to Epsom they would have trailed me to East Grinstead. Perhaps they had. But I doubted it. I'd been there most of the day, and it would have been the perfect place to take me out of the game. Quiet, deserted, with enough real estate to lose a dozen bodies.

Anyway, I'd been keeping a careful eye out. There was only one way – the old boy who'd told me. They must have got to him. I needed to go to the cottage again, but I needed to know how whoever it was had got to Natalie more.

So I pointed the nose of the car once more to the close where the Kellermans had been so brutally murdered. I drove right up to the front door of Southfork, got out of the car and rang the bell. Mrs Conway, Babs, answered.

'Hello,' she said. 'You again? How are you?'

'Fine,' I replied. 'Your gardener – is he about?'

'No. He didn't come in today.'

'Were you expecting him?'

'Yes. There's a lot of work to be done on the turf at the back.'

I'd been right. Jesus, not another body. I decided we'd talk landscape gardening another time. 'Have you tried him on the phone?'

'He's not on the phone. Who'd ring him?'

'Do you have his address?'

'Yes. But…'

'Can I have it?' I interrupted.

'I can't give it to you. I don't know you.'

Yes, I thought. But I bet we could have had a fuck the other afternoon. 'Babs,' I said, 'believe me, I mean him no harm. But there are people around who might. He told me something the other day. Something that might have a bearing on the Kellerman murders. I think these people might already have got to him. I just want to go and see if he's all right.'

'How do I know… ?'

'You don't. Just trust me. Give me the address. Please.'

I think it was the please that did it. 'It's in my book,' she said. 'Wait here.' She came back two minutes later holding a slip of paper in her hand. 'I've written it down.'

'Thanks,' I said. 'What's his name, by the way?'

'John. John the gardener.'

'Is that all?'

'Yes.'

'You don't know his surname?'

'I never asked.'

'OK, Babs.'

'I hope he's all right.'

'So do I.'

I went back to the car and drove towards South Norwood. With the aid of the *A-Z* I was at the street I wanted within about twenty minutes. John's address was on the corner opposite a big pub. I went up the three stone steps outside the front door and banged hard on the knocker.

A middle-aged woman in a flowered apron opened the door.

'What's all the noise about?' she demanded.

'I'm looking for John. John the gardener,' I said.

'You're in a hurry,' she said acidly. 'Are you late with planting your hardy annuals?'

I ignored her sarcasm. 'Is he in?'

'No.'

My heart sank. 'Do you know where he is?'

'If he's not here, he's at work. If he's not here or at work, he's in the pub over there.' She pointed across the road. 'With the other wasters. Public bar.'

'Thanks,' I said, and walked down the steps again and crossed the street. It was an old-fashioned boozer, still split into 'Public', 'Saloon' and 'Lounge' bars. I pushed through the door with PUBLIC BAR cut into the glass panel at the top. It was small, dingy and nearly empty. John the gardener was sitting on a stool at the bar itself. He looked like he'd already had a few over the eight. I hadn't been so relieved to see anyone for a long time. I went over and tapped him on the shoulder. He looked round and blearily up at me. In front of him were the remains of two pints and what looked like a large Scotch.

'What?' he said.

'Hello, John,' I said. 'Remember me?'

I saw the bulb go on over his head. 'Hello, son,' he said, suddenly all friendly. 'Have a drink.'

'No, thanks,' I said. 'Aren't you at work today?'

'No,' he said, breathing fumes into my face. 'I talked to your mate. He was more generous than you.'

'My mate?' I said.

'Yeah, he came by the other morning. Told me you'd sent him. Gave me a hundred nicker.'

'What did you tell him?'

'What I told you.'

'About the girl in the car with the sticker on it?'

'Yeah. It was all right, wasn't it?'

I wasn't about to tell him what had happened to Natalie. It

wasn't his fault. Any more than it was Jim's. Or mine. Or maybe more mine than anyone else's. Who knows? 'It was all right,' I said.

'A hundred nicker,' said John, almost disbelievingly. 'That's more than I earn in two weeks from that cow. She can stuff her sodding garden.'

'What did he look like?'

'Who?'

'My mate.'

'Yellow hair. Tall. Blue coat. Don't you know?'

'Course I do. Just checking.'

'He is your mate, isn't he?'

'Course he is. He didn't give you his name by any chance?'

'No, I don't believe he did. Are you sure you won't have a drink?'

'Go on then,' I said. 'I'll have a half.'

There was nobody about behind the bar. John banged on the counter. 'Service,' he shouted. Nothing. 'Bastards,' he said, and banged again.

A minute later, a middle-aged woman with a worried face came in from the back. 'Is nobody serving you, John? I am sorry. Where's Alfred?'

'In the bloody cellar, where else?' said John.

'I swear he spends half his life down there,' said the woman.

'I expect he's got a secret tunnel down there, to some tart's house,' said John.

And suddenly I knew what was wrong with the cottage in East Grinstead. 'Forget the drink, John,' I said. 'I just remembered somewhere I should be.'

'Are you sure, son?'

'Yes,' I replied. 'And I think Mrs Conway is worried about her turf.'

'Sod her turf,' he said.

'I think that might be the idea,' I said, and left.

30

I got into the car and drove to East Grinstead again. I was beginning to feel like a commuter.

The evening traffic was snarled all the way, and the Granada began to overheat. Typical of one of Charlie's clunkers. But eventually I turned off the main road and drove past the cottage.

I stopped well out of the way, just in case there'd been any other visitors in my absence. I cut across the orchard and into the lane at the side of the building. There were no fresh tyre tracks in the damp earth.

Good sign.

I went to the front of the house and stood in the shadow of an over-grown privet hedge.

Everything looked quiet. And empty.

I walked up to the door and let myself in silently. Inside the place had a deserted feel. Just like I'd left it. I went through the cottage in less than a minute. No one had been there since I'd left it days before, I was sure of that. Nothing had been disturbed that I hadn't disturbed. So Natalie hadn't told. She'd killed herself first. I wondered if I would have been so brave. Or maybe it had just been the last of many straws for her. The final indignity in a lifetime of indignities.

I could still see her eyes staring lifelessly at the wall. Wherever she was, I hoped she was free now. Free to walk. Free to run.

I went out to the shed in the garden. Just as I remembered, there was a big retractable tape measure in a leather case on one of the shelves. I went back and measured the kitchen and the cellar.

That was it.

The cellar, which looked like it ran the length and breadth of the cottage, was about four feet short at the back. Under the living room.

I tapped the walls again. They still sounded solid. Then I looked closer. I went over every inch of them. Every square centimetre of plaster and brick.

It took me hours to find it. I pushed, pulled, twisted everything I could find to push, pull and twist, until I'd ripped off three nails and the skin on the tips of my fingers was like sandpaper.

It had to be there, and it had to be easy. You just had to know how.

I went to the light switch at the top of the stairs and fiddled about with it. I even went into the living room above to see if there was a trapdoor in the floor.

Finally, when I was just about to give up, I tried the rose in the ceiling where the single bulb was housed.

That was it. I turned it once right, then left and right again, and one section of the wall in front of me opened silently. Sweet, David, I thought. Well sweet. And I walked over to the door I'd found, and looked inside.

It was dark, but I found a switch and turned it on. Another single, bare bulb came on to reveal a small fortune.

It was a blagger's dream inside the little room I'd found. A thieves' paradise.

There was money everywhere. Stacks of it. Solid blocks of

fivers, tenners, twenties, fifties, all neatly banded and piled against one wall, to the height of a tall man, and about two feet deep. There were cartons full of loose money too. Baked bean cartons, beer cartons, crisp cartons. In one corner was a mountain of coins that reached almost to the ceiling. Some in off-white cotton sacks, some in clear plastic bags, marked with the amount inside and the denomination of the coin. Some loose. Like it had just been shovelled there as too much trouble to count.

The floor was carpeted with empty money bags. From Barclays, Nat West, Lloyds, and most other major banks and building societies. There were night safe bags, boxes marked with the name of security firms, and jewellery display cases and ring trays. There were cartons full of jewellery too. Rings, necklaces, bracelets, mixed in together in a mess of gold, silver, platinum and precious stones. There was one box with just Rolex and Cartier watches. No Taiwan fakes either. These were all in their cute little velvet-lined boxes, with their guarantees still intact. I pushed my hands into one carton of tom. It gleamed and glittered in the light from the bare bulb in the ceiling. The stuff was heavy and cold and slippery as I lifted a double handful.

I found the deeds to the cottage. They were in an old cardboard file on top of a carton full of cash. Along with cheque and paying-in books in the name of Donald King. And Access, Visa and American Express cards in the same name. In one of the pockets of the file was a British passport. Just one. Name: Donald King. Photograph: David Kellerman.

In another corner, up against the wall, stood a canvas gun case. Next to it was a leather holdall. I unzipped the case. Inside was a Savage 20-gauge, four-shot, pumpaction shotgun. I worked the pump. Smooth as silk. A real rock 'n' roller's dream. I opened the holdall and found a hammer-shrouded Colt detective Special, still in its factory packing, a box of .38 ammunition, another box with shells for the Savage, and a comprehensive gun cleaning kit.

So Robber had been right. Kellerman/King was dirty. Very

dirty. And Webb too? I didn't know. And the others? The mystery men who'd been following me? Were they the rest of a gang of over-the-pavement merchants led by Kellerman? Almost certainly. Some part of this loot was theirs, and that's what they'd been looking for.

Christ, but my head was beginning to ache again.

I took the Colt out of its box, and wiped the excess gun oil off it with a soft rag from the cleaning kit. Then I loaded both the pistol and the shotgun and put extra ammunition for them in the pocket of my jacket.

I took the guns and went upstairs and sat on the sofa in the cold darkness of the sitting room and tried to think. Tried to put it all together in my head with the help of a two-thirds-full bottle of Scotch from the tray of spirits, and the remains of my packet of Silk Cut.

By then it was late. Very late. Too late for some, but just the right time for others.

With the information I had, and some supposition on my part, I came up with about as many questions as answers. But this is how I worked it out: James Webb calls me in to find out who killed his sister's family. He's all cut up about it. Or is he? Did he actually employ me to find the murderers, or to recover the take from what looked like a series of very lucrative robberies that his brother-in-law had stashed away?

Not that it was all the take. It couldn't have been. Andrew Cunningham, Kellerman's accountant, had told me that there had been too much cash floating around the business for a long time. Suddenly there was too little. So presumably Kellerman had been laundering money for quite a while. The cash and jewellery downstairs must have been the skim that he had appropriated from the rest of the gang for his own use. A bit like trying to steal a fillet steak out of a shark's jaws.

So whilst Kellerman's playing this dangerous game, he's building up a fake identity for himself. Just himself. Then he buys a remote cottage for himself and his lover to live in and uses his building skills to construct somewhere to hide the skim. Owing to an unfortunate oversight on his part, the cottage doesn't suit the lover, who happens to be wheelchair bound.

So Kellerman buys another house but doesn't sell the cottage and tells his lover that it's 'an investment for the future'. Some investment. A real hedge against inflation.

There had to be a million quid's worth down in the cellar.

Then he buys the second house, the bungalow in Epsom. He puts it in Natalie Hooper's name and settles a large amount of money on her. Almost as if he knows he might not be around for long. Either he's ready to take it on his toes *or* he suspects that he's close to the Big Au Revoir. Maybe he realises that sooner or later the gang is going to go down the river for a long time, and him with them, or that they're beginning to suspect he's been double-crossing them.

Now no one knows, or apparently even suspects, that Kellerman has a lover. The pair of them manage to keep it dark for years, mainly because Natalie Hooper is in a wheelchair. And like she said, most people only see the chair and not the person inside it. So after Kellerman's death no one considers that she might know where the goodies are hidden.

And what about her? Did she know or guess what had been going on? Had she conned me into coming here? I didn't think so. All my instincts told me she was being straight when she'd told me her story. She was in love with the geezer and that was that. If she knew where the stuff was, or even thought she knew and wanted me to find it, why didn't she just tell me? If she was going to get her hands on it, she'd have to tell someone eventually. She couldn't get to it on her own. She couldn't even get in the house. No, I stuck with my original feeling. She was on the level.

But *someone* was taking the piss, and I didn't like it.

Common sense said call in the law, turn what I'd discovered over to them and bow out gracefully.

But then, whenever did I listen to common sense?

I finished the bottle and tossed it into the fireplace next to the empty vodka bottle from the other day, and the butts of the cigarettes I'd smoked. My mouth felt like crap and the headache had arrived good and proper.

Eventually I must have dropped off into a fitful sleep. I woke up feeling grimy and gritty-eyed. I couldn't remember when I'd last washed or changed my clothes. It was five in the morning and light.

I went upstairs and had a lick and a promise in cold water in the bathroom. Then I went back down to the cellar and closed the secret door. I didn't touch the money. Like Kellerman and his gang, it was dirty. Tainted with too much blood. I wanted no part of it. I locked the front door behind me and went back to my car.

I took out the back seat and hid the guns and spare ammunition under it. I had a feeling they might get some use before long.

31

I stopped for something to eat at a Little Chef on the main road. It had just opened. I was the first customer.

I had an all-day breakfast with toast and three pots of tea. Not bad. Nor were the waitresses. But they steered well clear of me. I thought that I must be losing my sex appeal. How right I was. When I went to the men's room and looked in the mirror I wasn't surprised they were wary. I'd seen better-looking things squashed on the side of the road. The case was beginning to get to me.

I left a decent tip to make up for the view and drove back to town.

I went straight home. You know what they say. It's somewhere they've got to let you in.

I hoped that the Indian family had been keeping Cat's calorie count up. I needn't have worried. He was outside the front door when I bumped the Granada on to the front of the house. Fat as a rat, and pleased to see me.

I checked my mail. Just bills. The flat itself was secure and I opened a window to let some fresh air in. There were no strange cars in the street, and no one had nailed a dead chicken to the door.

I showered and changed into fresh clothes, and my other pair of Doc Marten's. I made some tea. Whilst the kettle was boiling I tried Fiona's number. Her answerphone was on. She was probably still asleep. I left a message, asking her to ring when she got up.

I took the tea and sat on the bed. I was whacked. I put the mug on the bedside table, leaned back and closed my eyes for a second.

The telephone woke me with a start. The sun had moved to the centre of the sky. The tea was stone cold, and Cat was asleep on my chest breathing curry into my face.

I looked at my watch. It was past noon.

Outstanding behaviour.

I picked up the receiver. 'Sharman,' I said.

'Tony Keogan,' a man's voice said.

I was suddenly wide awake. 'What? How the hell did you get this number?'

'It wasn't exactly difficult,' he said. 'I've been looking forward to speaking to you for a long time, Mr Sharman.' His voice was light but cultured. Just what you'd expect from a brief. Even a failed one.

'I can't say that the feeling is mutual.'

'I'm sorry to hear it. And I can see you're a man who has no time to waste on idle chit-chat. So let's get straight down to business. I believe you know the whereabouts of – how can I put it? – certain assets that belong to my business associates and myself.'

'And what makes you think that?'

'Just a feeling I have.'

'I hope you and your feeling are very happy together.'

He ignored my comment. 'What did Natalie tell you?' he asked.

'Wouldn't you like to know?'

'Of course I would. That's precisely why I'm asking.'

'And I'm not telling.'

'I'm afraid I must insist.'

'Go to hell.'

'I'll pass the message on to Judith and Fiona.'

I went cold all over. I actually felt the goose bumps breaking out on my flesh. 'What did you say?' I said.

'Judith and Fiona. You do know their names, don't you? A beautiful couple of young women. You must be very proud of them.'

'I don't know what the hell you're talking about.'

His voice hardened. 'You shouldn't have left them on their own. But you did. And now they're with us. And here they'll stay until we get our money.'

'Where are they?' I demanded.

'They're safe. For now. But the more time goes by, the less safe they become. *Capisce?*'

'How do I know...?'

'Hold the line,' he said. The phone went dead.

My hand was shaking. I watched it shake, like it belonged to someone else. 'Nick,' said Fiona's voice. She hardly ever called me Nick. 'For Christ's sake, do what he says. He'll kill us if you don't.' The phone went dead again.

Then Keogan came back on the line. 'Satisfied?' he said.

'If you hurt either one of them, I'll kill you, I promise,' I said.

'You're not in any position to make threats, Mr Sharman, so I suggest you save your breath. However, I can assure you that at the moment they're both in A1 condition. Now I think that we should meet, don't you?'

'Yes,' I said. 'I'd like that fine.'

'Alone and unarmed, Mr Sharman. No tricks. No games. No police. Or no daughter and no girlfriend. Do I make myself clear?'

'Perfectly.'

'Park your car outside Brixton tube station in half an hour,' he said. 'Don't be late. Remember, punctuality is the politeness of princes.' And he hung up.

32

I parked illegally outside Brixton tube station at ten to one. The entrance reminded me of an ant's nest that someone had stamped on. Crowds of people were streaming in and out and flying off in all directions. No one looked like they were enjoying it. The white faces were ghostly pale, and even the black ones appeared grey in the afternoon light.

On the pavement outside the station were Socialist Workers selling newspapers, Militants selling newspapers, Marxists selling their rag, Rastas selling posters of Haile Selassie and Bob Marley, New-age hippies selling joss sticks and love-beads, several scruffy-looking trucks flogging overpriced hamburgers and ice-cream, flower sellers, a newspaper man, people giving out leaflets for gigs or free haircuts, beggars, winos, all sorts. It was like bloody Delhi. At least no one was showing their sores or amputations. Not yet. Stick around, it has to happen.

I watched one guy marching up and down, up and down, like he was fixated. He was dressed in filthy denims. His hair was stiff with dirt, and his skin crusted with grime so thick it was like warpaint. He was clutching a beer can and shouting and hollering at nothing in particular. His coordination was all out of whack.

He kept stepping over imaginary obstacles between the paving stones. Mental health care within the community, I thought. I should bloody cocoa! He was flying on instruments only, and looking for a place to crash land. People coming out of the tube were looking at him nervously and hoping it wasn't them he was going to pick on when he came out of orbit.

I was so busy clocking the poor bastard that I almost forgot why I was there, and didn't see a figure come up behind the car until he hunkered down and tapped on the window beside me. Christ, it made me jump. I turned and his head was less than a foot away from mine. Disconcerting that. He had a ratty face with fine blond hair that didn't look as if it would be around much longer. All I could see of his clothes, him squatting down to see through the window, was a clean white shirt, narrow black tie and a navy overcoat with the collar half up.

Keogan, without a doubt. I rolled down my window. 'Sharman?' he checked.

I nodded.

'Stay calm,' he said. He let the overcoat open and put his hand inside on to the butt of a gun in a shoulder holster. 'They're both all right.' He went round and got into the passenger seat next to me. He took out the gun as he got into the car. It was a Ruger Standard Auto. Only .22 calibre, but it would do the job. He could hardly miss from where he was sitting. He held it down out of sight of the street, but pointing in my direction. 'I assume you weren't foolish enough to come armed,' he said.

'No,' I said. The guns I'd taken from the cottage were still underneath the back seat. Hardly ideal for a quick draw.

'Or told the police.'

'No,' I said again.

'I hope you're telling me the truth.'

'I am. I realise that you hold most of the cards.'

'But not all,' he said.

'No,' I agreed. 'Not all.'

'And what do you propose to do about that?'

'You tell me.'

'I will,' he said. 'You give me what I want. I'll give you what you want. We'll all be happy.'

I couldn't remember the last time I'd been happy. 'What then?' I asked.

'Drive,' he said.

'Where?'

'Just drive. And slowly.'

I touched the ignition and the engine caught. I put the gear stick into drive, indicated, checked the mirror, and when there was a gap in the traffic, turned the wheel and gave the car some gas. I headed down towards the Town Hall.

'What have you done to them?' I said. I was trying to stay calm, but I was still shaking and my knuckles were white on the steering wheel. This was turning out to be one of the worst days of my life.

'Nothing,' Keogan said.

I crossed the light by the Ritzy. 'Where now?'

'Tulse Hill.'

I kept to the left-hand lane, and accelerated past the old synagogue where the car breakers' yard is now. 'I said, keep it slow,' he said.

'If you don't tell me what you want, I'll wreck this fucker and you with it,' I said through clenched teeth.

I felt the metal of the gun barrel on my neck above my shirt collar. 'Try, and you die right now,' he said. 'Then you'll never see them again. I'll take my chance. If anything happens to me, the pair of them are dead. Now, slow down.'

Reluctantly, I did as I was told.

I drove through the next set of lights by The George Canning and up Tulse Hill. He turned and looked behind us. I glanced in the mirror. The road was empty. 'Pull into the flats on the left,' he said.

I slowed down and obeyed him. 'Park over there.' He pointed

to where he meant. I stopped in a gap between two blocks that backed on to Brockwell Park. The estate was deserted at that hour. 'Switch off and give me the keys.'

I did as I was told. 'Now get out of the car and stand where I can see you.' I opened the door, got out and walked to the front of the car. Through the windscreen I saw him open the glove compartment, feel under the dash and seat, and even pull down the sun visors. He didn't look in the back. Just as well. He got out and came over and patted me down. 'Fine,' he said. We got back in the car. 'Just drive round,' he said. 'Like before. Nice and slow, so we can talk.' He gave me back the keys. I started the car and steered it out of the flats and up Tulse Hill.

'What exactly do you want?' I said.

'Our money.'

'Why are you so sure there is any?'

'We know. And we're right, aren't we?'

What was the point? 'Yes,' I said.

I saw him grin. Like a shark. 'A lot?'

'Yes,' I said again.

'I knew it.'

'And if you get it back, what then?'

'Then you get your girlfriend and daughter back.'

'Simple as that?' I said.

'Of course.'

'And if I give you what you want, you kill all of us. Like you killed the Kellermans. It was you, wasn't it?'

'He was a bloody fool,' said Keogan dismissively. 'You're not. We had a good deal going, but he wanted more.'

'But why kill them? Why go that far? You might have lost the money forever.'

'These things happen. They're not always planned. One of our little côterie went over the top. Lenny. Big fellow. Rather overpowering. I think you've met.'

'He was driving the Volvo?'

'That's right. He's something of a loose cannon. We couldn't stop him. It was unfortunate. A bluff can only be called so far. David Kellerman called his bluff. He didn't think that Lenny would shoot. He thought wrong.'

'And now he's got my daughter.'

'Yes. But she's quite all right, I told you that. Just don't call our bluff and she'll stay all right. Calm down and keep driving.' He seemed to be enjoying himself. 'Now, where were we?'

'How did you find out he was doing you over?' I asked. I was interested to see if my suppositions had been correct. Maybe it wasn't the time or place, but we didn't seem to be going anywhere special, and as long as we were talking, he wasn't going to be killing anyone.

'We'd had our suspicions for a long time.'

'How long had it been going on?'

'What? Him turning us over?'

'No. The blagging. The robberies.'

'How did you know about that?'

'I guessed,' I said. And I'd been right. 'So how long?' I asked again.

'Years,' he replied. 'He was a slippery little swine. But, by God, he was good at what he did.'

'Which was?'

'Money Man. Organiser. Fixer. Planner. Architect. Call it what you like. He set them up and we knocked them over. Christ, we had some fun. Audacious, that was David. Audacious. You wouldn't believe some of the jobs we did.'

'And he laundered the dough through his firm?' I asked.

'That's right. And anything else we got he fenced off. He was quite brilliant. A great loss.'

'But he started robbing the robbers?'

'He had to spoil it. It's criminal the things people do.'

I had to agree.

'And we told him we knew. We spelled it out for him. But he

wouldn't have it. Kept on about additional expenses incurred, and cash flow problems, and the recession in the retail trade. As if we gave a damn about that. If we cared about the retail trade, we'd've all got jobs at Safeway's long ago, wouldn't we?'

I had to agree again.

'But *he* was never short. That wife of his never had any "cash flow problems". She always got what she wanted. A new car every six months. It's all right for some, isn't it? All *we* wanted was what was ours.'

'And?'

'And he wouldn't cough. Excuses, that's all we heard, excuses. So we did something about it. We warned him. We told him straight what would happen if he didn't come across. But would he listen? No, he wouldn't. And I'm telling you the same. So don't ever say that I didn't.'

Perish the thought. 'It was a bit drastic, wasn't it?' I asked.

'What?'

'What you did.'

Keogan considered that one for a moment. 'Could be,' he said. 'But sometimes that's the way it goes.'

'You see,' I said, 'it makes me think that if I do have something you want, and I give it to you, you might be a bit drastic with me and my daughter and my girlfriend afterwards.'

'No. Not if you give it up. Just tell us where it is and we can all part friends.'

'That's what you say now.'

'Look, I give you my word. Give us the money and we're out of your life. If anything we'd be grateful. We're not heartless people. We don't want to hurt your little girl or your girlfriend. But just in case you're the type to bear a grudge about it, and just in case *you* get any ideas, we've told a few of our friends about you. If anything should happen to us, or ours, they'll be round to see you. Just give us what you've got and we can all forget about the whole matter. Put it down to experience.'

With his word and a nicker, I could get a cup of coffee.

'Sounds cosy,' I said.

'Listen, Sharman,' he said, leaning forward until his mouth was close to my ear, and the gun was just tickling my kidneys. 'Most of us are family men, and none of us is getting any younger. We don't want this aggravation. We worked hard for that money and we want it. We know it's somewhere, and you know where that somewhere is. Just tell us and we can all get on with our lives.'

'So was Kellerman,' I said.

'What?'

'A family man.'

'He took the piss,' said Keogan. 'He asked for it. The rest of them got in the way. Don't you ask for it. All right?'

'What about Natalie Hooper?' I asked. 'Did she take the piss too?'

'That was unfortunate,' said Keogan sadly. 'She had this mistaken notion of loyalty. We weren't going to hurt her. We even let her use the toilet when she said she needed to. Then she locked herself in and by the time we got in after her, she'd killed herself. It was horrible. She had no need to do that.' He sounded quite offended.

'What matters is that she told us she'd put you on to something. Something we didn't know about. A place they used to go. That's right, isn't it?'

There was no point in denying it. 'That's right.'

'But she wouldn't tell us where. Why did she tell you, do you think?'

'I asked the right questions,' I said.

'You must have done.'

'Did she know about Kellerman?' I asked.

'What about him?'

'What he was up to?'

'No.'

'But you told her, didn't you? You had to tell her.'

'Yes.'

'Then she killed herself.'

'That's right. I mean, who would have thought it? Her and David. It's strange the things that people do.'

'And how about Webb?' I asked.

'How about him?'

'Was he with you? On the robberies?'

'Jimmy?' said Keogan. 'Hardly. Definite lack of bottle there. I think he got it knocked out of him in the ring.'

'Why did you put him on to me?'

'Sorry?'

'In the first place. Why get him to hire me?'

'Because he was rushing round like a crazy man. As time went by and the police got nowhere, he was determined to put *someone* on the case.'

'But he offered you the job. Why didn't you take it? You're an enquiry agent, aren't you? You could have lost in a fast shuffle, and looked for the money at the same time.'

'Not really. I run that place to keep the tax man happy. My main income comes from other things. Unrelated things.'

I could imagine.

'Of course I was looking, all the time. But it was too close to home. I didn't want to get too involved with the police. I thought that if I started sticking my nose into their business they might stick theirs into mine. And that would never do. And he would never have given up. Never.'

'But why me?'

'Why not? You're local. You've solved things in the past for people. And you did well. You found exactly what we wanted.'

Some reference, I thought. Another one for the old CV. 'So why kill Stan McKilkenney?'

'Old scores being settled, I'm afraid. We wanted you to find our money, not nail us for the killings. Lenny knew Stan of old. It's a very close-knit community around that part of the world, as you well know. And no one loves a grass.' He looked over at me with half a smile on his face. I was going to knock that smile right off. Very soon. 'We followed you that day,' he said.

'I know.'

'And we thought we were so discreet.'

'You said it wasn't your line,' I said. 'Enquiry work. You were right. I spotted you a mile off.'

'Why didn't you do anything about it?'

'I thought you were someone else.'

'Too bad.'

'Too bad for Stan.'

'True. We couldn't believe it when you met him. Then he started to ask around. I'm afraid we couldn't have that. Lenny suspected that Stan had had a hand in putting one of his cousins away. He decided to kill two birds with one stone. I told you he was a loose cannon.'

'You're telling me an awful lot,' I said.

'And you're not going to do a thing about it. You have a hostage to fortune. If anything happens to us that appears to emanate from you, your little girl is going to regret it. Maybe not immediately, but sooner or later. I hate to make threats like this but I'm afraid I must. I can't emphasise enough how dangerous it would be for you to talk. Just give us what we want and walk away. Believe me, it's no big deal. You'll give it up in the end. Do it without the pain.'

I sucked my teeth, then spoke. 'OK,' I said. 'Let's do it.'

'I knew that you were a reasonable man,' said Keogan.

'The exchange could be difficult,' I said.

'No. Not if we all have each other's best interests at heart. And trust each other.'

Trust. Now there's a word.

'Where and when?' I said.

'Later today. Of course, we'll have to be sure that what you say's there, is there.'

'It's there,' I said.

'Where exactly?'

'At a cottage near East Grinstead. I'll give you the details when I see Fiona and Judith and know they're OK. I'll give you the address and directions.'

'We could all go there.'

'I don't think so. It's a little too secluded for my taste. When we swap, I want to be in plain sight.'

'Where then?'

I thought for a minute. 'You'll have to get someone down there.'

'No problem,' he said.

'And when they've seen it's kosher, they'll have to get in touch. But I warn you, the phone is off.'

'No problem again,' he said, and took a portable phone from his coat pocket. 'We've got several of these.'

I bet he had a fax machine too.

'Good,' I said. 'That makes life easier.' I slowed the car and took one hand off the wheel and felt in my jacket pocket for the key to the cottage and gave it to Keogan. 'Get someone down to East Grinstead for six. When they're on the A22 on the other side of the town, get them to phone you. Bring Fiona and Judith. When I see they're safe, I give you the address and directions. He'll be there in a few minutes. As soon as he's satisfied, he phones back and that's that. OK?'

'Sounds reasonable. Where do we meet?'

'The concourse at Waterloo Station. Under the clock.'

'Are you crazy?'

'No. Like I said, somewhere in plain sight.'

'I'll think about it.'

'Don't take too long. Like you said, we've got to trust each other.'

'I'll call you after four,' he said.

'Do that.'

'Now drive me back to Brixton.'

I did as he said. When I stopped at the lights opposite the tube, he jumped out and vanished into the crowd. I looked at my watch. It was almost two.

33

I drove straight to James Webb's house in Crystal Palace. I didn't have a lot of time but I wanted to see him. Besides, it would keep my mind off Fiona and Judith. He was home. He was always home it seemed. He let me in and showed me into the same room as Judith and I had been the previous day.

'You look rough,' he said. 'Where have you been? I've been trying your phone.'

It was the wrong thing to say. 'Rough?' I said. 'You'd feel fucking rough too, Jim, if you were me. Just be thankful you're not.'

'I don't know what you mean.'

So I told him about Judith and Fiona being kidnapped. When I'd finished, his face was ashen and he sat down on the sofa. 'Oh, Christ, I'm sorry,' he said. 'I had no idea.'

'How much of an idea did you have, Jim?' I asked.

'Do what?'

'Don't "do what?" me,' I said. 'If I thought you knew what's been going on, I'd kill you here and now.'

'I don't know what you're talking about, I swear.'

Jesus, I thought. He doesn't know what I'm talking about. 'Have you got a drink, Jim?' I asked.

'What? Yes. What do you want?'

'A brandy would be good.'

He got up and went to the cabinet, and poured me a large shot of VSOP. I took the glass off him and he sat down again.

Then I told him exactly what I'd been talking about. I laid it out for him as I paced up and down his maroon shag pile in that comfortable room in that comfortable house in that comfortable suburb where he lived.

'Your brother-in-law was a fixer for a gang of blaggers, Jim,' I said. 'Stop me if you don't know what I mean by that.' He said nothing. 'He fronted the money for armed robberies all over the south-east. He'd been doing it for years. He didn't go over the pavement himself, but he sussed out, planned, and organised the robberies. Then, if it was cash that was stolen, he laundered it through his carpet business. Anything else he fenced off. It financed that lovely house of his, and your sister's dishwasher, and put the boys through private school. It was a sweet deal. It could have gone on for years. It did go on for years. But two things happened to turn it sour. I don't know which happened first, and it really doesn't matter. One, he got involved with a woman.'

'What?' said Webb.

'He had an affair.'

'Who with?' Webb interrupted.

I smiled. The smile didn't feel right, so I stopped. 'Natalie Hooper. His secretary, PA, whatever she was.'

'Natalie!' he said. I knew it would be a big surprise.

I nodded.

'But...'

'Save it, Jim.' I said. 'Don't give me the reasons why it couldn't happen. Believe me, it did. It had been going on for two or three years.'

'But I had no idea.'

'You weren't supposed to.'

'What was the other thing?'

'What?' I said. I'd lost the plot. 'Oh, yeah,' I remembered. 'Two, he got greedy. He started taking some of the stolen money, jewellery, whatever, off the top. He used some of it to buy a cottage in the country. Supposedly for him and Natalie to live happily ever after in. He was a bit of a do-it-yourself merchant, wasn't he?'

Webb nodded.

'He built a secret room in the cellar to keep the money and stuff hidden away. But Natalie couldn't live in the cottage. It was all wrong for her, what with the chair and all. So he bought her another house. A bungalow in Epsom. He didn't do any DIY there. He didn't need to. He put the place in Epsom in her name, and gave her a bunch of money to live on. More proceeds from the robberies, I imagine. That was when the carpet game started to suffer. Even though the robbery business must have been going well, his expenses were getting high and I think he was planning to get lost somewhere, and needed all the readies he could get his hands on.'

'I knew nothing about other properties,' said Webb.

'You weren't supposed to. No one was. Only him and Natalie. Oh, I didn't tell you, did I? He bought the cottage under a fake name. Donald King. Sound familiar?'

He shook his head.

'He'd built up a whole identity under that name. I found bankbooks and credit cards and a passport in the name of King in the secret room in the cottage.'

'It's still there?' he said. He sounded surprised. I suppose I would have been too, under the circumstances.

I nodded. 'Untouched from before he was killed until I discovered it yesterday.'

'Christ! How did you find it?'

'Natalie Hooper told me about it.'

'She knew?'

'She knew about the cottage. She didn't know about his extracurricular activities.'

'You wait till I see her.'

'You don't want to, Jim, believe me.'

'What do you mean?'

'She's dead.'

'What? How?'

'She killed herself. Slashed her wrist.'

'Where? When?'

His questions were coming in tandem. I looked at him. He'd said I looked rough when I came in. He should use a mirror. He looked terrible himself. Ten years older than when I'd first met him just a few weeks before.

'Epsom,' I said. 'In the bathroom of the bungalow David Kellerman bought for her, a couple of days ago.'

'Why? After all this time.'

'She had other visitors.'

'Who?'

'The rest of your brother-in-law's little firm. The men who killed him and his family.'

Webb looked shell-shocked. 'You know who they are?'

'Some of them. Keogan for one. Your mate.'

He shook his head. 'I can't believe…'

'Believe it. Plus there's a big geezer called Lenny, and at least one other. Ring any bells?'

He shook his head.

'Lenny was the one that shot at Judith and me yesterday.'

'How did they get on to Natalie?'

'Give me a break, Jim. You told Keogan over the smoked salmon mousse that I'd found an old boy doing the gardening opposite your brother-in-law's house. An old boy who gave me a lead. The lead was to Natalie. The old boy told him too. Keogan told him I was his mate. *You* put them on to Natalie.'

It was just as well he was sitting down, or he'd have fallen down. The blood drained from his face and he put his head in his hands.

I didn't feel a bit sorry for him. Not then.

'Oh, God,' he said. 'I didn't know. You've got to believe me. I didn't know.' I believed him. 'And the bastard's got your daughter?'

I nodded.

'Why?'

'Why do you think? He wants to make a trade.'

'For the money you found?'

'Sure.'

'And then they'll leave you alone?'

'So they say now. But I'm thinking that they might decide that anyone who knows anything might be better off dead.'

'So?'

'So I'm between a rock and a hard place, Jim. Two innocent people are involved. I can't be with them forever. Every morning when I wake up, I've got to wonder, is this the day? Is this the day they come looking for us to make sure we *never* talk?'

'So what are you going to do?'

'Give them what they want. Then go in and blow them away.'

'Have you got a gun?'

'A couple. In the car. They were at the cottage.'

He went over to the bureau by the wall and opened a drawer. When he turned round he had a gun in his hand.

'Christ!' I said. 'Where the fuck did you get that?'

'I'm in the sports business, Nick. I told you that, didn't I?'

I nodded.

'I import a lot of stuff from the States.'

'You told me that too.'

'Sometimes I import guns, under licence.'

'Show,' I said, and reached out my hand.

He gave me the gun. It weighed a ton. It was an Iver Johnson Cattleman. It looked like a Colt Peacemaker. I thumbed out the loading gate, quarter cocked the gun and checked the cylinder. It was fully loaded.

'Forty-four?' I asked.

'Yes.'

233

'The gun that won the West. What were you going to do with this? Shoot buffalo?' I handed it back to him, and he went over and put it in the drawer again.

'If you found out who killed Sandy, I was going to kill them myself,' he said as he turned away from the bureau.

I looked him in the face. 'Would you have, Jim? Would you really?'

'Maybe. I'm not sure.'

'Then you wouldn't.'

'I don't know.' He looked at me. 'I'm not scared of going to prison.'

'I am.'

'I'm not.'

'Why not?'

'Because I'm dying.'

'Who isn't?' It seemed to me lately that everyone was dying or dead.

'You don't understand. I'm dying *now*.'

'What's the matter with you?'

'Cancer.' he said. 'That's why I was going to shoot them. I've got nothing to lose.' He tapped his chest. 'I've got a time bomb ticking away in here. It's about ready to go off. That's why I wanted someone private to look into it. Even if the police *were* still working on finding those bastards, I didn't have time to wait. I needed some action before it was too late.'

'You got some.'

'I knew you were my last chance.'

'I'm glad I didn't disappoint you.'

'You didn't.'

'I wish you'd left it alone.'

'I couldn't.'

'Why not? What was the point? Because of you more people are dead. And more are going to die before it's over.'

'I couldn't,' he repeated.

'But why?'

'Do you believe in the afterlife?' he asked.

'No,' I said.

'I do. I couldn't face Sandy and David and the boys without trying to get them justice first.'

People were always talking about justice for the dead. I wondered about justice for the living.

'If I'd shot them, I wouldn't have gone to prison for it,' he said.

He looked so sad and sick as he spoke, that I actually felt sorry for him. 'How long have you got?' I asked.

'A few months. Weeks maybe.'

There was nothing to say to that. I lit a cigarette and looked for an ashtray. There wasn't one. I dropped the ash on the carpet.

'When are you going to do it?' he asked.

'Tonight. After the swap. It has to be. It's the only time I know they'll all be together. And where.'

'Why not send in the police?'

'It doesn't work like that, Jim,' I said. 'If they're nicked and it's down to me, they'll keep coming. I have to do it this way. Afterwards, what happens happens. Maybe Keogan was lying. Maybe it'll be all over. If not...' I didn't finish the sentence.

'I'll drive you,' he replied. 'I'll help.'

I thought about it for a second. 'All right, Jim. You can come. But leave the howitzer at home.'

'OK.'

'I warn you, it's going to get bad.'

He didn't reply and I let it go.

I explained what I'd arranged with Keogan about getting Fiona and Judith back, and that I was waiting for confirmation. I told him I'd call him after I'd been to Waterloo if everything went according to plan. When I'd finished I said, 'Sure you still want to come?'

'Of course. Give me one of those, will you?'

'What?'

'A cigarette.'

'I thought you didn't.'

'It doesn't matter now.'

I lit him a cigarette and he pulled hard on it. 'First one for six years,' he said.

'Smoking can cause fatal diseases,' I said.

He laughed a hollow laugh. 'It's a bit late to worry about that now.'

It's funny. You don't like someone much. Then they say something. And maybe it's what they say, or maybe it's the way they say it. But you suddenly realise that you've been wrong. That was how I felt about Webb then. I wished I could have a chance to know him better. But I knew I couldn't. I just left him a couple of cigarettes and said goodbye.

34

I left Jim and went back home to wait for the call from Keogan. I didn't have to wait long. He phoned at 4.30. 'It's on,' he said. 'I'll meet you under the clock at six. But I warn you, no tricks or those two are dead.'

'I'm not playing tricks,' I replied. 'I just want them back. You can have your sodding money, and welcome. But I want to see them before I tell you where it is.'

'You'll see them,' he said, and cut the connection.

Just before five I went out to the Granada and took the Colt from under the back seat and put it in the pocket of my leather jacket. It wasn't beyond the bounds of possibility that Keogan would be the one playing tricks, and I wanted at least one ace. I drove the car to Waterloo, waited for a parking slot to come free in the thirty-minute zone on the covered ramp that ran down to York Road, reversed the car into the slot and went into the station. At that hour on a weekday it was bloody chaos. That suited me fine.

I walked round the edge of the concourse looking for suspicious characters. By the time I'd gone ten yards I'd seen dozens. I checked my watch. 5.35. I went over to one of the fast-food concessions with clear sight of the area under the clock and bought a coffee. I stood leaning against the front drinking it and smoking a cigarette, keeping an eye on the big picture.

Keogan appeared like a puff of dark smoke at 5.59 precisely. I dropped the styrofoam cup into a trash can and walked towards him. He was turning on his heel, looking nervous. I didn't blame him. There could have been a hundred armed police within twenty yards of him and he wouldn't have known. He saw me coming and relaxed. I kept my hands away from my body, just in case he had a minder near. Armed.

'Where are they?' I asked as I got up to him.

'Close.'

'Show me.'

He walked towards the back of the station. I followed. He went through the exit that led to the open car park down by Lower Marsh. He took out his portable phone and tapped in a number. It was answered straight away. He whispered something and cut off the call. Thirty seconds later a red Sierra estate came up from the car park, stopped about a hundred yards from where we were standing, and both front doors opened. Lenny and another bloke I didn't recognise got out and opened the rear doors. Judith and Fiona emerged from the back of the car and stood looking at me.

'Satisfied?' said Keogan.

'OK,' I said, and told him what he wanted to know: the whereabouts of the cottage, and the way to get into the hidden room.

He punched another number on the pad of the phone and relayed the information.

Then we waited.

The minutes dragged. Five. Ten. The six of us stood like a tableau whilst the world passed us by, completely oblivious to what we were doing.

I put my hand inside my pocket on to the butt of the Colt. I looked up. The sky was lavender-coloured again and weighed down on me like iron.

The phone in Keogan's hand purred. He answered it with a terse, 'Yes,' then listened. When he cut it off he looked at me triumphantly. 'Good,' he said. 'Very good.'

'Have you got what you want?' I asked.

'Definitely.'

'Then let them go.'

'I said I would, didn't I? But remember, any tricks and you'll never have a peaceful day again.'

'I realise that,' I said.

'OK, Sharman,' he said. 'Wait here.'

He walked over to the Sierra and spoke to the two men. All three got into the car and it pulled away, leaving Fiona and Judith standing in the roadway.

I turned and watched it go, then walked over to where they were waiting.

35

Both of them looked stressed out, tired and dirty. Judith's eyes were red from crying. The look in Fiona's was something else again. As I got close she came towards me and hit me in the face so hard with her closed right fist it felt like my cheekbone was fractured. Then she slapped me with her other hand. I grabbed her wrists and she twisted in my grip. 'Fiona, no,' I said.

People stopped and looked. We ignored them. 'Not here,' I said.

'You bastard,' she hissed through bloodless lips.

I let go of her wrists and went to Judith. I knelt and hugged her. She was so stiff in my arms it was like holding a statue. I looked over her shoulder and then closed my eyes. When I opened them, the world was still black. As black as I've ever known it.

I stood up and took Judith's hand. 'The car's round the corner,' I said to Fiona.

We walked to it in silence.

I unlocked the doors and let Judith into the back. Fiona got into the passenger seat. I got in behind the wheel and half turned in the seat and looked at both of them. My face hurt like hell where Fiona had hit me.

I was the first to speak. 'Are you two all right?' I said.

Fiona shot me a look of pure contempt. 'Yes, but no thanks to you, you stupid bastard. You couldn't leave it alone, could you?'

I said nothing in reply but looked at Judith sitting in the back. She looked straight ahead at something no one else could see and I realised that what I'd allowed to happen had gone beyond the limits of where I could expect forgiveness. I'd gone over the edge and was falling fast.

'For Christ's sake, why? Didn't you realise the kind of people you were dealing with?' demanded Fiona.

'It was something Wanda said.'

'Fuck Wanda. She's dead. What's she got to do with it?'

'You wouldn't understand.'

'Of course I wouldn't,' she said. 'I'm fucking stupid, aren't I? But I understand what happened to us. I understand how close we came to being killed. I know you don't care about yourself, Sharman. And frankly I don't care any more if you care about me. But what about Judith? She was terrified.'

'Did they do anything to you?' I asked.

'Like what?' said Fiona.'

'You know.'

'Spit it out, Nick,' she said, and there was an anger and hardness in her voice I'd never heard before. 'Did they rape us? Is that what you're asking? Did they interfere with our maidenly honour? Is that what you're so worried about?'

'Yes,' I said.

'No. But one of them talked about it. If you didn't come across with what they wanted.'

'Which one?' I asked.'

'You're pathetic,' she spat.

'Which one?' I repeated. 'Just tell me.'

'I see,' she said. 'You've got it all worked out, haven't you? You're going to go and hurt him. Fuck what happened to your daughter. Just so that your honour's satisfied. Your sorry little macho pose is safe. Pathetic! Jesus, I don't know why I ever bothered with you.'

'Just tell me, Fiona,' I said. 'I want to know.'

She sighed. 'The small one in the car just now, with the hooded top,' she said. 'Satisfied?'

'Fine,' I said. I turned round and leaned over into the back. 'Were you frightened?' I asked Judith. Stupid question.

'Yes, I was.'

'I'm sorry. It was my fault.'

She looked at me for the first time. 'No, it wasn't, Daddy.'

Christ! After all she'd been through, she could still say that. I felt ashamed; a great wave of shame, like a pain in my gut, and a hot flush of anger for the men who'd put her through such an ordeal.

'It was because of me,' I said.

'That doesn't make it your fault.'

'That's a matter of opinion, sweetheart.'

'You can say that again,' said Fiona.

I started the car. 'I'll take you home.'

'And?' said Fiona.

'I'll come in and see that you're safe. Then I'm going out again for a bit.'

'Are you fucking serious?' said Fiona.

'Yes.'

'Aren't you going to stay with us?' she asked.

'No.'

'You're just going to leave us?'

I didn't say anything.

'You're a bastard, Sharman. We need you. Judith needs you.'

'I know. I'll be back later.'

'Later is too late for me.'

'Judith?' I said, looking over my shoulder.

She sat in the back, little and white-faced and hunched up like an old woman. I felt that pain in my gut again. 'Judith?' I said again.

She looked at me. 'You will come?'

'Of course,' I said.

'I'll be fine,' she said.

'Good girl,' I said. Patronising git.

Fiona said something ugly under her breath. I didn't blame her.

'I'll be back tonight,' I said. Or never, I thought. Maybe that would be best for all concerned.

'When?' asked Fiona.

'Who knows?' I said. 'I'll be gone for a few hours. No longer.'

'What are you going to do?'

'I'm going to see Webb. The bloke who hired me in the first place.'

'And?'

'Who knows?' I lied.

'You're going after those men, aren't you?'

I shrugged.

'You'll get us all killed.'

I shrugged again, and put the car into gear and pulled out of the parking space, down the hill and into the main road. We were back in The Oval within ten minutes.

I went up to the flat with them. I asked what had happened, how Keogan and his crew had got them, but neither of them answered so I left it.

The flat was neat and tidy so I assumed that it had been outside. I wondered where Fiona's car was, but didn't ask. It would all come out in time, or it wouldn't.

All they would tell me was that there had been four of them: Keogan, Lenny, Hooded Sweat Shirt, and the one who'd been the passenger in the Volvo. That was really all I needed to know. We went into the kitchen and I put the kettle on and made tea. No one drank any.

It was that kind of situation.

I asked Judith if she wanted to go to bed.

'No,' she said. 'I want to stay with you.'

'Do you want a bath?'

She shook her head. 'Not now.'

I got a couple of beers out of the fridge and gave one to Fiona. I offered Judith orange juice. She shook her head again. We sat together in that silent kitchen for an hour. Then Fiona went and ran a bath.

'When are you going out?' said Judith when she had gone.

I looked at my watch. It was almost eight. 'Soon,' I said.

'You promise you'll come back?'

'I will,' I said.

Fiona was in the bathroom for half an hour. She came back in a bathrobe. 'Your turn,' she said to Judith. 'The water's just the way you like it. Lots of bubbles.'

Judith looked at each of us. 'You won't go until I come back, Daddy, will you?'

'Of course not.'

She left the room.

'Another beer?' I said to Fiona.

'Why not?'

I got two more out of the fridge. I didn't know what to say. 'I screwed up,' I said.

'That's nothing new.'

'I'll try and make up for it.'

'Don't tell me. Tell Judith.'

'You don't mind her staying here?'

'She's not going with you tonight, that's for sure.'

'I will be back.'

'Quite frankly, Nick, I couldn't care less.' She called me Nick again.

We didn't speak again.

Judith came back twenty minutes later.

'I'd better be going soon,' I said.

'Don't let us keep you,' said Fiona.

I got up and went to Judith. This time she held me tightly. 'I won't be long, darling,' I said.

I left then. I'd stayed longer than I'd meant to. The fact is I didn't want to go at all. Would you?

I got to James Webb's house at 9.45 and told him what had happened. Everything I knew. We left at 11.00. I took the shotgun from under the back seat of the Granada. He drove us in his Daimler.

36

We turned off the A22 just past East Grinstead on to the B2110. By then I could have done the journey blindfold. I showed Webb the entrance to the lane. He drove on for a couple of hundred yards until there was a place to pull off the road. He killed the lights and the engine. I collected the shotgun and got out of the car. It was chilly and quiet. There wasn't any other traffic on the secondary road.

'Come on,' I said. 'It's just over that field. And keep quiet. They might have somebody on watch.'

'All right,' he said. 'I want these bastards as badly as you do, you know.'

'Sorry, Jim,' I said. 'I forgot.' I pumped a round into the breech of the gun as we walked across the damp blacktop, over the fence and through the trees. The ground was soft underfoot but the moon was high and the way was clear. Within minutes we were at the fence that surrounded the garden. The front of the cottage was in darkness. We walked around to the back and I saw a single chink of light at the French windows. We climbed over the low fence and crept past the shed and across the wilderness that was the garden. There was no sign of anyone outside. Trust, you see. Or, more likely, greed.

Our feet were silent on the paving of the patio and I peered through the glass. There was a gap where the curtains hadn't been drawn properly and I could see one corner of the living room. Keogan was sitting on one of the straight-backed chairs, counting out a big pile of money on to the coffee table in front of the fireplace. The gun he'd held in the car was lying on the table in front of him. Lenny was standing behind him.

I couldn't see anyone else in the room. The other two had to be somewhere else in the cottage.

'I'm going in,' I hissed in Webb's ear. 'Stay cool, Jim.'

He wanted to say something to me, but I couldn't be bothered to start a conversation. I put my finger to my lips, shook my head and moved him away from the window. It was too late now. I leant my back against the wall, counted to three, and tried to get my mind right,.

I thought of Wanda, and what she'd said to me on her deathbed. I thought of the Kellermans blown to pieces in their comfortable house. I thought of Stan McKilkenney as he must have felt with a double-barrelled shotgun in his mouth as Lenny pulled the triggers, and Natalie Hooper as she inserted the sharp, cold blade of the razor into the soft, warm flesh of her wrist.

I thought of Fiona and Judith, caught up in a nightmare not of their own making, and I concentrated my entire being on the gun in my hands.

I spun round and blew the French windows to hell and gone.

The glass blew inwards with a satisfying crash and the curtains billowed and shredded and caught fire. I stepped through the frame and slapped the material out of the way.

Lenny stood like a statue in the middle of the room, his hands full of bank notes. I worked the action of the Savage, and blew a gaping hole in his stomach. He hit the wall hard and stood looking down at his guts smoking and running down the front of his trousers like wet, scarlet snakes. He dropped the money and tried to push some of the bloody bits back, but lost his balance and fell forward hard on to his face and lay quiet. I pumped another shell into the chamber of the shotgun. Keogan looked at the gun on the table.

'Go ahead,' I said. My voice sounded strange through ringing ears. He hesitated. 'Or don't,' I said. And I shot him in the chest anyway, and tumbled him and the chair he was sitting in across the room. The room was full of smoke and the smell of gunpowder and the stink of blood and flesh, suddenly and violently exposed to the air. I looked round. James Webb was standing in the ruins of the window frame. I chambered another round, then took a handful of cartridges from my pocket and replaced the shells I'd used. Then I went looking for the other two.

One of them was coming up the stairs from the cellar. He'd been the passenger in the Volvo. He was young and stupid-looking, but not for long. He was dead-looking before he knew it. I pumped the shotgun's action again, and looked down the stairs for the last of them, the one in the hooded sweat shirt who had frightened Judith so much. Nothing. All at once I heard footsteps on the stairs and the sound of a scuffle from the rear of the house. I turned back out of the kitchen and ran down the hall. I heard Webb shout: 'I've got him,' and I ran into the back room. It was carnage in there. Webb was holding the last man in an arm lock. 'Let him go,' I said.

He did as he was told. 'Step back,' I said again. Webb did as he was told again. I held the Savage in one hand and stuck the barrel under the fourth man's chin. He was sweating and shaking. 'Leave it out,' he said, almost choking.

'No,' I said back. '*You* leave it out.'

'What do you mean?'

'You're the one who likes to kill little boys and put it to little girls,' I said.

'No! It wasn't me. It was them,' he said desperately, pointing at the bodies on the floor.

'Yes, it was,' I said. 'And now I'm putting it to you. How does it feel?'

He tried to turn his head away, but I slapped it back with my free hand. 'How does it feel?' I asked again.

'I didn't mean it,' he said. 'I was only joking, I swear.'

'You're quite the fucking comedian, aren't you?' I said. 'Now you're going to die laughing.' And I pulled the trigger and blew his head clean off his shoulders. Blood and bone and brains and hair and gristle spattered the walls like impressionist art, and his headless body took two or three steps backward and fell half on and half off the sofa.

'Christ,' said Webb. 'Christ almighty.'

I threw the hot shotgun back through the doorway and looked at the money strewn around the place. 'The wages of sin,' I said.

'What are we going to do?' asked Webb.

'We've done it,' I said. And it felt good. But it wasn't over yet.

'Go out to the shed in the garden. There's a can of petrol next to the generator. Bring it in here,' I told Webb.

'What?'

'A can of petrol,' I said patiently. 'In the shed outside. Get it.'

'Why?'

'Work it out.'

He did as he was told. I stood and waited for him in that stinking room shaking like I had a tropical disease. I looked down. My DM'S were soaked with blood and the bottoms of my faded jeans were dark with the stuff. James Webb came back with the petrol can and gave it to me. I took the top off, and splashed the petrol around the walls and furniture and over the three dead men in the room, and along the hall and into the kitchen to the fourth body by the cellar door. I went back into the room where Webb was waiting and threw the last of the petrol up the ruined curtains and out on to the patio. I took out my lighter and thumbed the flint wheel. 'Say goodbye, Jim,' I said.

He said nothing, and I bent down and put the flame of the

lighter to the pool of petrol on the patio. It caught and the fire danced along the liquid, up the curtains and into the room.

'Come on,' I said. 'Let's get out of here.'

We ran along the lane and across the road to the car. As Webb pulled it away, I looked back once and saw an orange glow through the trees. I didn't bother to look back again. We headed towards Tunbridge Wells along deserted, sodium-lit carriageways, and picked up the London road just outside the town. Neither of us said a word until we were safely on the A21 and heading north. I was the first to break the silence. 'You can drop me off,' I said.

'Where?'

'The Oval will do.'

He nodded. 'Got another cigarette?' he asked. I lit two and left the pack on the dash. We didn't speak again on the ride back.

He stopped the car on the corner by the tube. 'Will this do?' he asked.

'Fine.'

'You don't have to worry, you know,' he said. 'About your daughter and your friend, or yourself. I'll take care of everything.'

'Is that right, Jim?' I said wearily.

He nodded.

'See you around then,' I said, and got out of the car and shut the door behind me. I watched his lights fade in the direction of Clapham before I headed towards Fiona's block. It was 2 a.m.

The cranky lift was working, and Fiona answered the door after I'd leant on the bell for a few minutes. 'Oh, it's you,' she said.

I felt about as welcome as head lice. 'Who were you expecting?' I asked.

She didn't answer. She had been in the big bed with Judith who was still asleep. She looked at the state of my clothes.

'You've had a busy night,' she said coldly.

I nodded. 'Have I got any clean clothes here? I asked.

'In the wardrobe in the bedroom. Don't wake Judith.' I went upstairs and found a fresh pair of jeans and a shirt. I looked at my daughter's face on the pillow of Fiona's bed as I left the room. She was asleep and dreaming. They didn't look like pleasant dreams. It was my fault. I went outside and changed on the landing. I took my bloodstained clothes downstairs and put them in the garbage. Fiona made me coffee, then went back to bed without another word. I sat in the living room and watched the dawn break over London with the Colt in my hand. I didn't sleep.

37

The fire at the cottage was the last item on the 5 o'clock news and each hourly bulletin after it on LBC. Fiona and Judith got up around nine. I turned off the radio. We didn't talk much. Fiona made eggs and toast for breakfast. I didn't eat. I was dog tired but still couldn't sleep. At midday I went out to get a paper. Things had changed since I'd last listened to the radio. The headline in the *Standard* read:

SHOTGUN MURDER BROTHER'S SUICIDE
Man kills four then himself

I took the paper into a pub and bought a bottle of lager and sat at an empty table in the nearly deserted saloon bar and read the whole story. This is what it said:

In an amazing development in the fifteen-month-old mystery of a bizarre murder in South London, James Webb (43), a company director of Cambridge Road, Crystal Palace, was found early this morning dying in his luxury car on the towpath of the Thames near Barnes Bridge, apparently from a self-inflicted gunshot wound.

Webb, a company director, was the brother of Sandra Kellerman (36), the mother of two discovered shot dead last March with her husband, carpet tycoon David Kellerman (45), and their children Toby (9) and Brian (6) at their million-pound mansion in Crown Point, South London.

Webb was rushed to Queen Mary's Hospital, Roehampton, but was dead on arrival according to a hospital spokesman. On the passenger seat of the car was a note. The police have not revealed the full contents, but a source said that Webb had named four men for the murders of his sister and her family, and had admitted shooting them dead earlier last night at a remote cottage near East Grinstead, and then setting fire to the building. He also indicated that the men were part of a gang who successfully executed a series of daring robberies at banks, jewellers' and other premises in the Home Counties, over a period of several years until the death of his brother-in-law, whom he also named as leader of the gang.

Police have declined to confirm or deny the incident, but local reports from East Grinstead indicate that the emergency services were called to a suspicious blaze that completely destroyed a building outside the village of Coleman's Hatch in the early hours of this morning. The building has since been cordoned off and forensic experts are waiting for the ashes to cool before they can carry out a detailed search of the ruins. James Webb's wife, Mrs Doreen Webb (39), was not at the family's luxury £500,000 house this morning, and police say she is staying with relatives at an unspecified locale. Neighbours in the quiet, tree-lined street expressed shock and amazement at Webb's alleged suicide.

The piece went on with a resumé of the story of the murder in Crown Point. I folded up the paper, lit a cigarette and finished my drink. Jim had come good, like he'd promised. And all the time he'd had his gun with him, and never said a word. I went to the bar, ordered a triple brandy and raised a toast to him with it.

If there was an afterlife, as he believed, he'd be with the ones he loved now. I hoped he was happy. Say hello to Wanda and Natalie and Stan for me, I thought.

I finished the brandy and went back to the flat, and showed the paper to Fiona. 'Looks like you're off the hook,' she said.

'Looks like we all are.'

'You'd better take Judith home then,' she said.

'Yes, I'd better,' I said, and I did.

About Us

In addition to No Exit Press, Oldcastle Books has a number of other imprints, including Pulp! The Classics, Kamera Books, Creative Essentials, Pocket Essentials and High Stakes Publishing > oldcastlebooks.co.uk

For more information about Crime Books go to > crimetime.co.uk

Checkout the kamera film salon for independent, arthouse and world cinema > kamera.co.uk

For more information, media enquiries and review copies please contact Frances > frances@oldcastlebooks.com